I0667145

galley proof

ERIC ARVIN

Dreamspinner Press

Published by
Dreamspinner Press
382 NE 191st Street #88329
Miami, FL 33179-3899, USA
http://www.dreamspinnerpress.com/

Galley Proof

Cover Art by Anne Cain   annecain.art@gmail.com
Cover Design by Mara McKennen

ISBN: 978-1-61372-333-3

Printed in the United States of America
First Edition
January 2012

eBook edition available
eBook ISBN: 978-1-61372-334-0

To Miranda, Maxie, Jack, and Mugsy,
for letting me use their beautiful home as a setting for this book.

a room of one's own

I WAS clearly caught in a cliché.

Everyone has seen those films—usually a sex comedy about high school or college—in which an alluring character is introduced to the plot with the use of soft lighting, swoony music, and, depending on the level of writing, induced drooling from the other characters in the film. Said character enters the library or cafeteria and the music hits its stride. Every other character, but most notably the main character, is dumbfounded—nay, lobotomized—by the sheer sensuality and godlike nature of that which has just walked in. Life, we are led to believe, was nothing before this divine event.

Yet what we aren't privy to as viewers of this type of film—not at the outset, anyway—is what trouble will follow in this beauty's wake. And there *must* be trouble, for without it there is no story. No life. No box office. What boisterous, if unbelievable, shenanigans will the hero have to go through to get the guy or girl of his or her dreams? And will it be worth it? That's what makes or breaks films like this: worth. For if it is worth it, if after all the embarrassing smackdowns, the disgusting flatulence jokes, and the strained one-liners, if in the end we really do care about these somewhat contrived and clichéd characters, then we can forgive any plot hole. We, every one of us, are only looking for a good time, after all. Nobody expects a romcom to change their life.

Logan Brandish. That's my real name. I was destined to be a writer, it seems, with a name like that. And I'm a decently successful writer too. I have even managed to amass a firm little nest egg from what was, at one time, a dubious career choice. Even when my sales start to sag, I'm still successful enough that my publisher, Hillside Books, pays for my meals at posh hotel restaurants. Especially when they want me to meet with a new editor.

And, now that introductions are out of the way, so starts my tale.

To put it plainly, I was pigging out. My new editor had yet to arrive and I had already ordered half the menu and was on my second Long Island Iced Tea. I'm a pretty man—clean-cut brown hair, a face that has been described as "open," and a body that knows its way around a gym—but I don't know how pretty I was looking just then. Though, in my defense, all thirteen dishes on the table were in nice rows, perfectly laid out. I was a stickler for order and conformity.

Normally when meeting with an editor, I would arrive early to look over my notes for my new project. But my notes had been destroyed. By me. In a fit of anger and self-ridicule. All that was left was a single piece of paper, which now lay on the table, a small dab of shrimp cocktail sauce on the right corner. Who cares.

It was for precisely this reason, I suppose, my publisher at Hillside Books decided to send me a new editor. They could tell I was having issues and thought maybe an editor could help. This is when editors start to resemble mean drill sergeants. There were going to be some major battles in the coming weeks and months. Most likely their thinking was that if they started things out between me and this new editor, a Mr. Brock Kimble, in a chic hotel restaurant where there were other people around, things would not so quickly dissolve into a sparring match—like it had with the last editor they sent me. And honestly, I've never been one for showy displays of anger, so they thought correctly. I was not going to knock over the gorgeous pastry tables or throw dishes at the large crystal chandelier, even if the thought did cross my mind. I was a nice guy. I would not be throwing the wine into the cascading fountain or slap some passing waitress across the face just for being too near to me. But I had decided I would not be so easily soothed either. Yes, I would eat their free food and drink their bribery wine, but I'd be damned if I gave Mr. Kimble one smile. My tolerance was worn thin already. Like that Kool-Aid T-shirt I had kept since high school and refused to throw away. Worn thin.

No. Mr. Kimble would have to get by on my curt and dismissive answers and challenging stares. I was very proud of myself for deciding all of this. It was written like a script in my brain.

And then, as I was devouring a chicken wing as if doling out vengeance, my moment of cliché happened. Into the restaurant walked what could only be described (albeit inadequately) as a stunning man. I swear, the room went silent and everything crawled in his presence. He was dressed in a dark suit, buttoned properly so that it showed a tapered waist. His shoulders were broad, and above them, *oh deliciousness*, was a face so proportioned and perfect I wanted to take up drawing on the spot. His hair was dark, as were his eyes. In fact, he was so pretty I found myself gagging. Then I realized that the chicken wing was still crammed halfway down my throat. Silly me. I spat it out just as his eyes focused on mine. The chicken landed on the plate with a resounding echo and my face, I could tell via the flames of my embarrassment, was flushed. My ears were most likely bright red as well.

I began to chant to myself: *Please don't be him. Please don't be him. Please, please, please don't be him.*

But it was. And he was soon standing over me, grinning. He looked at my table and the mess I had made. "You've been busy," he said. "Cute ears."

As I reached for his offered hand to shake it, I gasped and choked. A bit of leftover chicken flew out of my mouth and onto the table, in front of his crotch. Humiliation complete. Lesson learned.

"Sorry," I said, taking a quick drink of water. People were looking at me disapprovingly for daring to nearly die in public.

"Don't worry about it." He smiled and sat down, sitting his briefcase in the seat beside him. "I've had worse things thrown at me than a piece of regurgitated chicken. I'm Brock Kimble."

"Logan Brandish. Of course, you know that, or you wouldn't have known how to find me. Wish I had had a photo of you." I grimaced. That did not sound right, even though the implication was very near the mark. By golly! He was pretty!

"Would have been easy enough to find you. All writers have the same look of social discomfort and inferiority."

Wait. What?

I can only imagine what I must have looked like, sitting there with him. How others saw me. He ordered his drink with style. He did everything with style. He was fluid. He was Henry Higgins. I wasn't even Eliza Doolittle. I was Nell, still choking up bits of chicken.

"*You're* my new editor?" I asked. My plan to be subtle and aloof was lost.

He must have heard that question and intonation before. His smile jarred the room. "I started as a cover model for the romance division of Hillside. After proving myself—he leaned in closer here, smelling clean and fresh—"and sleeping just a few feet up, I landed myself in this position. I've been in every position you can think of. Wink wink."

Wait. What?

Eyes bright. Eyes full of mischief. "I believe in being totally honest. That's one thing you should know about me, Mr. Brandish. Or Logan? I'll call you Logan. Over the next few weeks, I will hurt your feelings with some of my critiques, but I'll also be there to encourage you on. We'll get you going again. You'll see. I'll be like Henry V, ushering you on to victory... or something like that. I'm not certain what Henry V is famous for other than being played by Kenneth Brannagh. So, what have you got to show me?"

"Um... I... I'm having issues...."

He spread his arms. "That's why I'm here. You don't have *anything*?"

My fingers edged toward the lone, pathetic piece of stained paper on the table. He snatched it up and read it:

"*The trireme surged on the open sea.*"

He looked at the page a bit longer, then flipped it over as if there were any possibility at all of something being on the other side.

"This is it?"

"Well, there was more...."

"More better, or just more of the same?"

~ 5 ~

I didn't know how to answer that. The fact is, since the destruction of my notes, I had only gotten as far as the first sentence. Fifteen versions of the first sentence. (*There once was a trireme from Kent. Trireme Irene had seventeen children. Triremes are big, big boats powered by angry muscle bottoms. All aboard!*) The first sentence gets things going. It's the Start button to any new manuscript. Unfortunately for me, the first sentence of any new manuscript is like pushing a basketball out my urethra.

I shrugged and gave a half smile. That worked to get me out of trouble sometimes. I looked so all-American, people sang at me when the national anthem was played at ball games.

"Hmmm. Well, it's a start." He handed the paper back to me. "Do you know anything about galley ships?"

"No."

"Looks like you got some homework, then, huh?" He leaned forward and said, with a booming voice, "'Cause I sure as hell don't either, and have no intention of edumicatin' myself about 'em. Know what I mean, Jelly Bean?"

He was a silly man. A silly, gorgeous man.

A handsome young waiter brought Mr. Kimble his drink and I noticed a lingering gaze between the two. That's when my stomach dropped and my balls disappeared into my abdomen. Here was a lovely gay man and I had, quite purposely, sabotaged any chance I had with him. He had even said I had cute ears. I had most likely put him off eating for the rest of his life with the whole chicken debacle. He certainly wasn't ordering anything there. There wasn't room left on the table.

The waiter looked at me, disinterested, and asked if I needed anything more.

Go away, little bird. Go away.

"I've read your blog," Brock said. "Very entertaining. Witty."

"Well, I'm no Noel Coward."

"Never heard of him. Unfortunate name. About your blog. Like I said, entertaining stuff, but I would reconsider the links to the naughtier sites. You know. The porn blogs and naked men."

How dare he!

"We want the focus to be on you. We don't want anyone who has come to your site to be distracted by pretty pictures. We want them to stick around and not be clicking away for the first pair of fresh ass cheeks they see." About that time, a fresh pair—those of our handsome young waiter—walked right by. Mr. Brock Kimble couldn't keep himself from following them for just a bit.

"It's my blog. It's like a diary. I post things that interest me."

"I get it. I know what a blog is. Still, the Lord wouldn't like it."

My jaw literally dropped.

"Just kidding." What a wicked smile.

He looked around the restaurant for that cute little waiter. The one I had just bitch-slapped in my mind. "But seriously, consider taking those links down."

"Are we through here?" I asked, doing my best to show some irritation.

"Sure. Would you like me to help you clean up?"

"No, I would not! I don't think I like you, Mr. Kimble."

"Good. Then you can stop worrying about how you appear around me."

I froze. How could he know? How could he tell how awkward I felt?

His eyes locked with those of the waiter. "I've got another meeting," he said. "And you've got homework."

I sat a while longer, trying not to pay attention to my new agent walking out the door with the waiter. In my most Walter Mitty-like fantasies, I swung into action and knocked the waiter on his cute little buns. He was fired for flirting with a customer and trying to steal my man, and then Mr. Kimble and I purchased a suite where we fucked like toys wound too tightly. My fantasy love life was always so exciting. But life never measured up to fantasy. In real life, kisses are never as sweet and assholes only stretch so far.

I LIVED in a big Victorian house on a shaded street in the small town of Adbury with my best friend, Janey Caster. We met in college and became very close almost immediately. We tapped into each other's needs quickly. The neighborhood we lived in was nice. Upscale but not snooty, and not a lot of children. There was a garden out back of the house, which we tried to keep alive. Over a short, white fence, we traded gardening tips with the feisty old woman next door, a Mrs. Grace Allenson. Nice old thing, if somewhat nosey. She could be a bit Margaret Rutherford at times. Janey and I had a Persian mix named Feed the Cat. We thought we were terribly clever when we named her. Janey was drunk at the time. Me, I have no excuse.

To our occasional delight, the street itself—East Second Street—seemed to be in the middle of a territorial dispute between the Mormons and the Jehovah's Witnesses. It was ridiculous, outlandish, and—we were convinced—totally true. Sometimes there would be a set of each of the two faiths on opposite sides of the street. Mrs. Allenson watched them as if she were watching a prizefight.

"Look at 'em eyeing each other," she'd said once while we stood talking over the fence in the front yard. "Do ya suppose we're going to have a holy dustup?"

And it was true. As far-fetched as it sounds, I half expected them to break out in song and click their fingers, like some reject *West Side Story*.

I walked into the house and found Janey right where I expected: sitting on her feet on the couch at the window and watching a set of nicely monotoned Mormons knocking on doors across the street. Feed the Cat was curled up beside her in a spot of afternoon sunlight that had snuck in past the tree branches. Janey was in her favorite blue shorts and a slim white T-shirt. Her shoulder-length hair was pulled up into a sloppy, auburn ponytail and she held a half-eaten Snickers like a rabbit's foot. She loved Snickers. Milky Ways, though, made her gag. Who knows why.

"Hey, baby," she said, not taking her eyes off the Mormons. "Can you believe this? They totally skipped our house again. Why do they keep doing that?"

"I honestly don't mind it." I sighed, as if I had been doing strenuous work all day. As if I had come in from the fields.

"Well, I do! We haven't had a Mormon or Jehovah's Witness come to our door since we bought this place. Why the hell not? We're just as sinful as everybody else. Why aren't they

trying to convert me? I'm offended by the whole damn thing."
She ripped at her candy bar.

"Go tell them. You might want to get out of your comfy
clothes, though, and into something more presentable."

"I'll give them some more time to come around. Maybe this
is just buildup. Maybe I'm so sinful they realize they will need to
pull out all the stops."

"I bet that's it." I plopped down on the couch beside her.
Feed the Cat looked at me with annoyance.

Janey was not the type to be ignored. When she wanted
something, she usually got it, and with insurance. She had found
out just a year before that a movie star from the 1930s, of the
Irene Dunne ilk, grew up in an old house just down the street
from us. The house was falling apart and forgotten. Janey
hounded the historical society until they spent the money to fix it
up again, reasoning that it might just be a wonderful tourist
attraction. Film nuts would love it. "She's been nominated for
five Oscars!" she had screamed at the head of the board, a
pretentiously religious woman named Della who also happened to
be a lawyer. "How many have *you* got?" Della eventually caved,
but not before Janey riffed on her in the local paper as being of
the law firm of Jesus, Mary & Joseph.

"How was your meeting with the new editor?" she asked.
She had a narrow face. Delicate, with large green eyes. She could
be precious or she could be manipulative.

"I don't like him. He's very pretty, but I don't like him."

"I feel the same about these Mormons. They're very pretty,
but I don't like them."

The fact was, however, I would have given my right nut to
be the one leaving the restaurant with Mr. Brock Kimble.

Thinking about him, about that fine body beneath that fine suit, tented my khakis. I felt Feed the Cat staring at me. Judging.

"Curtis is on his way over," I said, rising from the couch. "Tell him I'm up in my room."

"Absolutely. I don't want him down here with me whilst I'm stalking. He'd bring the whole mood down."

"Janey, he's not that bad."

"Logan, darling, your boyfriend is mind-numbing." She sat properly on the couch and faced me. "Last week he cornered me in the kitchen and gave a whole speech on the fascinating topic of cardboard boxes."

Yes. I was dating a cardboard-box maker. About as interesting as it sounds. We had met when I needed a box to send ten signed copies of one of my books to my mother, Lucille. Everyone in her circle of friends demanded a signed copy of all of my books. If she remembered to give them out, well, that's another matter. But Curtis was there at the store that day to help me out, and so began our tangleweed romance.

"He's a sweet man," I said, and turned for the stairs.

Curtis Little. King of Little Boxes Big Store. And that's all I knew of it. Even my trips to his store had been a blur. Cardboard boxes. I mean, who cares? I always reminded myself he was a very sweet man. That had to count for something. Better sweet than abrasive, like the gorgeous Mr. Brock Kimble. I adjusted my hard-on in my khakis as I entered my bedroom.

My bedroom had been converted by me, from the library or office it had originally been when whoever built the place lived there, to something quite a bit less severe. Or at least the effort was there. There is really only so much one can do to make bigness seem cozy. The room had a tall ceiling, crown molding, and two large windows. Opposite the windows, two dark oak bookcases spread out from a corner axis like arms in invitation to read. They were lined with books, notes, and anything else I didn't have a proper place for. Everything was neatly in place and easy to find. Books in alphabetical order by author, CDs by artist. I had a desk directly beneath the bookcases, where I wrote on my laptop. In the other corner of the room was where I slept, on an old sleigh bed that came with the house. I tried not to think of the phantom sex that had occurred on that bed, but, after all, it wasn't like it was the same mattress.

I turned on my laptop and played at writing.

Ten minutes later, Curtis stood in my doorway. He was dressed in browns and whites, as usual. Curtis would not enter a room unless asked, and he would never make himself known with a cough, so if I hadn't seen him standing there, he might have stood perfectly still for ten minutes more. He easily faded into the wood. He might have said something to get my attention, but his voice was so light at times it's doubtful I would have heard him from my corner of the large room.

He was a pleasant-looking guy. Nothing stunning. Nothing hideous. He was just there. He was Curtis and he always wore a smile and was constantly setting his glasses on his nose. His hair was short and neat. His nose whistled sometimes when he found something humorous. Physically, he had but one attribute that stood out. It bubbled, rather. His rear. He had a very nice, very round butt, and he knew how to show it off without ever really *knowing* how to show it off.

I smiled. "Come on in, Curtis." When we spoke I noticed we often spoke in the manner of acquaintances. Not even friends. Acquaintances.

"How did I get the most talented, beautiful, most wonderful man in the entire state?" he said as he slouched in and gave me a kiss on the lips. "I brought you some of our new line."

He held up some small, flattened boxes. Curtis was always bringing me boxes. Sometimes they were even brightly colored.

"They're going to be big sellers." I had never seen someone get so excited about cardboard. He loved his job, as odd as that seemed to anyone who knew him. Curtis loved boxes.

I kissed him again, letting my hands wander down his back to that prized ass. I cupped it in my hands. I could feel him growing hard, but whether that was my doing or his thinking of boxes I cannot say. At the moment I didn't care. In between kisses, Curtis continued talking in breathless whispers about his new box line. What they were made of, how strong they were, what colors they came in. I just wanted to fuck and, God bless it, his jabbering was getting in the way.

"There's a documentary airing on PBS tomorrow night about box making. We should watch it...."

I pushed him onto the bed and pulled on the elastic bands of his jockstrap, salivating at the thought of his ass. My fingers dug into him, squeezing plump life purple. That's what I wanted. Dangerous reds and violets. Bruised flesh.

"Ow!" he cried and stopped the proceedings immediately. "Honey, that hurt. Can we be a bit more gentle?"

Yes. He used the royal "we" often. It was like nails on a chalkboard to me.

"Sorry, sweetie," I said as I pulled down his pants and jockstrap with more tenderness but less excitement. My lust had been shaken.

He was hard. Curtis never disappointed in that area. And it was a very respectable dick. Just like him. Stiff and rigid and always eager to help. All it needed was a pair of eyeglasses. The problem, you see, was that Curtis was never too knowledgeable about how to use it. Now, I was never a Casanova, but I at least had a wonderful imagination. And Curtis? Well, Curtis liked boxes.

Still, I tried to work myself up once more. I stroked his penis a few times, giving it a quick flick of my tongue every so often, then gave his balls a gentle tug.

"Ow!" he cried again. "My scrotum! Baby, are you mad at me? Can't we just do this normally? Like we normally do."

Normally. Yes. Normal and safe and plain. That was Curtis. I smiled. "Sure."

And so we did. We did it exactly the way he wanted. And something in me clicked. Something I barely recognized until much later.

When Curtis left that evening, he seemed satisfied. I almost expected him to say "Good job, you!" with a pat on my head, as if I had done my duty. I rinsed my mouth out and got a drink. A night of nautical research awaited me.

As for my novels, I tried to write things that I knew at least a little bit about. College, small towns, neighbors, and so on. American life in the first days of this dangerous century told with satire and, hopefully, bite. It had not been my intent to graduate from college only to find myself in a career where I spent hours reading other people's words, other people's versions of facts about ancient seafarers. But there I was. Striking through the brush of the Internet with my invisible machete like I was E.L. Doctorow's slow brother or Mary Renault's jealous cousin. But if you're going to write historical fiction, you've got to have some historical facts. Unless you're Dan Brown.

That was mean. I know. But come on. As if he'll read this.

There is a lot on the Internet about ancient warships. Galleys, triremes, and the like. I hit all the major sites, looking for nuggets of interest. The truth is, though, no matter how interested you are in a subject, no matter how passionate, after a while it's just work. Every so often I would wander onto a page centering on erotica. The ancients make for great sexual imaginings. Time is the great fictionalist. M/M fiction, it's called. That kept my interest going for far longer than it should have. I was supposed to be researching, after all, not being turned on by muscle slaves and mean emperors.

Why had I chosen to write a novel of historical fiction on galley warships? I knew nothing of the ancient world other than what the History Channel had taught me, and I always had the feeling they weren't too terribly trustworthy. But then, history in the modern world is a painted-up muse resembling more a pop siren than any half-divine tart. If you want anything of substance, that calls for some digging. Why had I chosen a subject that forced me to do research?

Then I remembered: It was a wild hair. I wanted to try and *expand my horizons*. It sounds admirable when it's said, but when it's actually staring you in the face, it's a whole lot of expanse and you are too lazy for it.

I looked at the time. Two a.m. I decided to head for bed. I saved the few notes I had gathered from my research onto a flash drive and turned off the laptop. I leaned back in the chair and stretched. It would all begin again tomorrow, my precious routine. The same every day, with a few alterations here and there. My life revolved around lists and routines. They were tacked to the wall, folded in books, and saved on my laptop. Lists of things to do, places I wanted to see before I die, and, of course, outlines and half outlines for possible books. Sometimes I would find a list and I'd have forgotten what I even wrote it for. I had a lot of travel lists. I was not a traveler, but I always meant to be. I would save every list, no matter. You never know. You just never know. I'm a list hoarder, I suppose.

My daily routine was hung in my brain like it was boldly typed on bright white paper and then black-framed.

wake up (very important, this one)
stretch
check e-mails & messages
breakfast
watch the morning news (but not enough for it to ruin day)
work out (each day of the week having its own list of
particular exercises)
write until…
lunch
play on the Net, usually porn
cardio
write
some TV
dinner
write
coffee
chat online
get ready for bed
jack off

That's how it usually went every day. It was comforting and controlled. A big, deep breath. Curtis, of course, popped by, but he easily fit into the routine. That's why he was so perfect for me. He blended right in. Have I said that before? That he blended in.

Yet sometimes, and more so around that period of my life, when I lay alone in bed at night (Curtis rarely slept over), I wondered how my life could be different with different people, in a different place. Maybe someone like Mr. Brock Kimble in his perfectly fitted suit. Maybe in some place I've never been.

a swiftly tilting planet

Brockkimble: Are you there?

LoganBrand: Yes. I'm on. What's up?

Brockkimble: We need to make your book more gay.

LoganBrand: Huh?

Brockkimble: Yeah. You heard me. We need to gay it up. It's early yet, so we have plenty o' time to fix it.

LoganBrand: Fix what?

Brockkimble: Some of these notes and ideas you sent me… they're all well and good if you were going to write a buddy film. But this ain't Butch and Sundance. These guys are supposed to be in love, not BFFs. Take something you know about modern gay culture and transport it to then.

LoganBrand: I'll be honest, I'm not terribly familiar with what gay culture offers. I've not really done a lot.

Brockkimble: For instance?

LoganBrand: I've never been to a drag show.

Brockkimble: EVER?!

LoganBrand: Don't yell at me! Yes. Ever.

Brockkimble: What about dancing? Do you go out dancing?

LoganBrand: Absolutely not. Why would I do that?

Brockkimble: You are a gay, right?

LoganBrand: Not every gay man embraces all the clichés. There are plenty of us who are perfectly content to stay at home on Saturday nights.

Brockkimble: That's a lie!

LoganBrand: It's true.

Brockkimble: I won't believe it! I can't!

LoganBrand: I'm rolling my eyes at you now.

Brockkimble: The next thing you'll tell me is that you don't own any Diana Ross CDs!

LoganBrand: Please! If I have to hear "I'm Coming Out" one more time I'm going back *in*. I prefer Dylan over Diana.

Brockkimble: Downer, party of one. Your table is ready.

LoganBrand: LOL! Fuck off. So, I need to "gay things up," whatever that means. Fine. Is there anything else, O Mighty Editor?

Brockkimble: Fisting.

LoganBrand: Excuse me?!

Brockkimble: Fisting. Have you ever tried it?

LoganBrand: Hell, no! And why?! And have YOU?!

Brockkimble: I attempted it… once. I chickened out at the last minute. It's on my "to do" list.

LoganBrand: You are absolutely insane! There aren't enough drugs in the world to make me want to be someone's hand puppet!

Brockkimble: Calm down, Sphincter Sally! I wasn't asking if you wanted to do it. I was just thinking that is the kind of rough sex play that might be appropriate for the prisoners on your galley ship.

LoganBrand: Lots of fisting in ancient times, was there? That's a bit intense.

Brockkimble: Have you not seen *Caligula*? My point is, you need to dirty it up.

LoganBrand: Gay it up and dirty it up. So, the reading public is now filled with filthy perverts?

Brockkimble: You got it. So shock me, hooker. Make me think the worst of you.

LoganBrand: I don't want to do that!

Brockkimble: Ah, jeez! I don't even know who you are anymore!

LoganBrand: What?

Brockkimble: Nothing. Just a line from a movie. Quick question. Whose ass would you fuck first: Superman's or Batman's?

LoganBrand: Do you have some form of Tourette's where you ask completely inappropriate questions?

Brockkimble: I'd fuck Batman. Superman has all those superpowers. It's only logical that he'd have an impenetrable bunghole. I don't want to break the key trying to get it into the lock, if you get my meaning.

LoganBrand: And who knows if you'd ever get your wang back if you *did* manage to stick it in there, right?

Brockkimble: Now you're getting it!

LoganBrand: Have I any other choice?

A FEW weeks later I was again sitting opposite my new editor in the big city, this time at a small coffee shop of my choosing. The correspondence between Brock and me had been steady and nearly every day since our first meeting. I had never had an editor as nosy as Brock. Yet I wasn't annoyed by this. In fact, I began to look forward to his blunt observations and criticisms of my work. When he said he wanted to meet up again, face-to-face, my heart went into a strange gallop. It was lovely. I tried to tone down the excitement in my e-mail message, however. The night prior to our rendezvous—indeed, the whole day—I was a mess. Nerves, dear reader. Nerves. I decided I would wear brown cords and a nice shirt. I had decided this on the day Brock mentioned getting together in the e-mail. It was summer and perhaps a bit warm for corduroy, but they transformed my ass into art.

This time I made sure not to eat much at all while we sat discussing my writing. There was a blueberry scone on a plate in front of me, which he had ordered for me to go along with my half-empty cup of too-rich coffee, but I wasn't about to eat even a crumb of it. I was determined to leave a good impression this time. My stomach, however, made quite a fuss at this decision, rumbling and whining over anything that was said.

"You should eat something," Brock said. "I am concerned for your tummy. It is making the wildest of tummy noises."

He grinned. I blushed, then looked at my scone with unbridled lust. I wanted to fuck that scone.

"Go on. Eat it." Brock moved in closer over the table, seductively. His piercing eyes held me, as strong as if he had me in his arms. I wanted to fold. "Eat it all," he breathed out. He picked up his own scone (his third) and bit into it so ravenously I wondered that it didn't scream. In between those lips, I certainly would have.

I laughed and picked up the pastry, enjoying very much that first, wonderful taste. Unlike doughnuts, scones don't need to scream their tastiness with an overabundance of sugar.

"Now," Brock said. "About this manuscript." He looked down at the notes spread around the table. It was not a particularly encouraging look, and my heart sank. "I've read over what you sent me," he continued slowly. "So, it's a comedy? A spoof? Set on a galley warship?"

My defenses went up. "A romantic comedy. Yes. And it's not completely set on a galley ship. That's just the first part of it. A starting point. The characters have to have common ground. Some place or experiences that they both share to form a stronger connection."

"Uh-huh, uh-huh," Brock said too quickly. "But their names. Cummonus and Ejakulus?"

"It's a comedy!" I nearly yelled.

"Does it need to be so obvious? I mean, are you sure you have the skill for this? To carry this level of outrageousness through an entire book?"

I wanted to be angry with him. *Who was he?* Mr. Brock Kimble. Sitting there in front of me, with all his "perfect" hanging out for anyone to see. Yet the way he looked— the gentleness in the face, the perfect set of teeth, the cleft chin, the retro Dr. Pepper T-shirt stretched tightly, but not too tightly, over his wide chest—made me soften immediately when I felt like raging. Earlier, when he had risen to get yet another scone, that wonderful old T-shirt lovingly hugged his tapered V and led my eyes straight down to Brock's lovely rear, fitted in his faded jeans as beautifully as apples in their skins. Yes. I wanted to be quite perturbed with Brock's nonchalance, but I found my attention pointing me elsewhere.

"I half expected a musical number," Brock continued to deride my work. "And not a good one. Like a bad Mel Brooks number."

My stomach growled louder than I had heard it since childhood, when the bullies would take my lunch and I would starve through the school day.

"Don't growl at me. I'm just the messenger." He winked. "I'm just trying to make this the best it can be."

"I'm told I have a great sense of humor."

"I'm sure you do, Noel Coward, but this isn't what Hillside contracted you for."

"I know. I know." I put my hands to my forehead and rubbed. "I just can't get into it. Inspiration evades me."

"Would it help if you wrote in the first person?"

"Yuck. I hate first person." And that's true. I absolutely hate it. I wouldn't write in first person if you paid me.

Brock sighed. "I'm going to get you another scone. A whole plate of them if I have to, and we're going to figure this out. The galley ship is a good setting. You could have a lot of fun with this. I'm just not sure about the Brooksian comedy. I guess you could write it as is and we could try and pitch it to Broadway."

He rose and started singing "Proud Mary" in a deep, masculine voice as he rowed backward from the table to the barista. I had to laugh. How could I contain it?

DESPITE the laughter and a stomach full of scones and coffee, I came away from the meeting with Mr. Brock Kimble feeling defeated. I'm certain that was not his intent. What the hell gave me any right to call myself a writer? How had I managed to sell any books at all?

I remembered my first substantial published work. A ghostwritten memoir for my friend Cliff, a very popular gay porn star. The book was titled *Did I Shave My Ass For This?* It did very well and helped in getting me my first contract under my own name. I thought it was all going to be smooth and easy from there. But there were always times when I looked back at the things I have written that I thought, "This? This is what you've got to show for yourself?"

I remained friends with that porn star, by the way. He's in theater and bodybuilding now, but he doesn't act anymore.

One of the things I always did to get myself motivated to write if my muse was dragging was pick up a book by a favorite author—James Purdy or Jeanette Winterson or Geoff Ryman—flip it open to any page, and read for a few paragraphs. That usually got my creative juices flowing. But there exist some days when doing that would be akin to self-flagellation. There were and are some days, for me personally, when reading other people's brilliance does not inspire at all, but hinders. These wordsmiths castrate me with their greatness. How could I achieve such heights?

When I arrived home after the meeting with Brock, the house was quiet. Janey worked as a preschool teacher and wasn't yet home. I fed the cat and went up to my bedroom. At the desk, I opened my laptop to check my e-mail before getting back to my routine. There was a message from Mr. Brock Kimble. There were others, of course. Curtis's daily lunch greeting. A few messages on Facebook and Goodreads. But Brock's was the only name I truly saw. With a slight smile, I read the heading: DON'T GIVE UP... WHORE. He always knew just what to say. We had apparently reached a new point in our working relationship/friendship. The point when calling someone a "whore" becomes a term of endearment.

The body of the message was a cell-phone-recorded video. There he was, in the coffee shop. By the light around him I could ascertain he had recorded the message not long after I had left. He had most likely gotten the barista to hold the phone.

"You forgot your notes," he said, holding them up and smiling so gorgeously I forgot to breathe. "You can do this, Logan. Turn that spoof into truth! Give me a masterpiece!" Then he began to roll out of screen, once again singing "Proud Mary" in a deep voice that would have made an established over-actor blush and wince. He poked his head back on-screen for a brief moment. "I'll get it to you later!"

I watched it four more times before I heard Janey arriving home.

ADBURY was a quaint town that thrived on tourism. The storefront windows were meticulous displays of quilts, antique furniture, and such things of ages long since past that retain a chic interest to some. On most days in the summer, the doors of the stores were wide open, belching the crafts onto the sidewalks well into the evening. Janey and I decided to take a stroll after she got home from work. It was just after five. I was to meet Curtis back at the house around six. Mrs. Allenson had invited Curtis and me over for dinner. Janey had an argument with Della and the Historical Society to attend to later that night, so she would be unable to hear what would most likely be scintillating dinner conversation.

We window-shopped for the most part. Honestly, neither Janey nor I was the antiquing type, and crafts made us both shrug. Every so often we would see something that interested us in that same way one finds interest in a loom at a museum, but usually not enough awe was mustered to actually purchase anything. We had a few antiques in the house, but we were the practical sort. Substance over style. Streamlined.

We walked at a languid pace. The sidewalks allowed us this, being that not many people were out because of dinner and those who were had considerable age on us and were walking even slower than we were. We drank iced coffees from our favorite coffee place. Coffee shops, it seems, are to modern society what the baths were to the ancient Romans. They were everywhere.

"How's the new book coming?" she asked. She had yet to change out of her respectable school clothes. She would probably change before her Della encounter later that evening.

"I'm a terrible writer. It's dead. Dead, dead, dead."

"You'll fix it up. You always do. You're dependable that way."

"Dependable. Are you saying I'm predictable?" I gave her a playful and accusatory stare.

"Yes. But in a good way."

I was a box. A big, dependable box.

"At least I get to look at a sexy editor every now and then," I said. "That makes it easier. He sent me a video message today."

"Was it hot? Was he naked? Can I see?"

"Yes. No. And no." The truth was, I still felt flushed from watching the message. As if I had been caught watching porn. It was a feeling of adolescent guilt I had forgotten even existed.

"Why don't you ask him out?" She searched the bottom of her plastic cup with her straw for any remaining drops of deliciousness.

"What? No. I've got Curtis."

She looked at me with an arched eyebrow.

"Curtis is fine," I said. "Don't judge me. Curtis is just what I...."

Need? Want? What was the right word? It occurred to me that the thought itself didn't warrant a conclusion.

"He's just what you've settled for," Janey offered. "He's your safe ending, Mr. Writer, though I wouldn't say happy."

"Well, what about you? I don't see you dating anyone. Not for a while now. When will you get back in the game?"

"I was a star player in the game, if you remember correctly. I played hard. Too hard. I was the 'go to' girl. Not the 'I do' girl. Besides, no one's good enough for me. Have you any idea how hard it is to be as amazing as me? Any idea at all? I'm fucking fabulous. It really is a pleasure for people to meet me."

"You're waiting for one of those Jehovah's Witnesses or Mormons."

"There's an idea." As if it had never occurred to her. "I will get them in the house. Just you wait and see. I managed to get the attention of one of the Jehovah's Witnesses the other day. I was on the porch in the swing and this cute thing in a Walmart suit comes down the walk with a briefcase and a blond chick. I said 'hi' in hopes they would stop and try to convert me."

"Did they?"

Janey sighed. "No. The woman gave me a frightened look at the end of our sidewalk, and he must have thought I was flirting, because they scampered away like frightened salamanders. I didn't even get a tract from them."

"I'm sure you're in their prayers."

DINNER with Curtis, who showed up precisely on time, went as expected. It was pleasant and steady and, as usual, Mrs. Allenson—Grace to her friends—was a gracious hostess and had prepared a delicious meal of beef stew and fresh breads. For dessert, there was a lemon meringue pie in the center of the table, which Curtis was eyeing throughout dinner with more desire than he had ever eyed me. He was dressed nicely in a white button-up, khakis, and a tie. That was his life uniform. It's the look he always wore. If he ever wore any color, I never saw it. Still, he was dependable in how nice he looked. I felt underdressed in response, as I—inspired by Brock—wore my old Kool-Aid T-shirt and a pair of cargo shorts. But then, Grace was dressed in her jean overalls, so, in truth, Curtis was *over*dressed.

The conversation was mostly light. We discussed gardening tips and what latest controversy Janey had gotten herself into with the Historical Society. We discussed television programs we both followed and films we all loved. We discussed favorite cuss words. Grace liked *fuckery*. I preferred *assholery*. Curtis abstained from that part of the conversation, going bright red when asked. His eyes lit up, however, when he spoke of the box industry. Every long conversation with him always ended in a box. It was very cute to see for the first few moments. He looked as sweet as a puppy, all excited.

When we had arrived, he'd noticed a cardboard box filled with clothes for Goodwill. He mentioned to me then, as he mentioned to Grace now, how it was a competitor's box and they weren't very strong. "Let me bring you some good strong boxes," he said. "I'll drop them by tomorrow."

"Thanks, honey," Grace replied. "But I can't say as I need any more boxes." She poured him some more wine.

"Everybody needs boxes!"

I tried to come to Grace's aid. "Maybe she doesn't have the room."

"Did you know," he said, continuing as if I hadn't said anything at all, "that the cardboard box was invented in 1890 by a Scotsman living in Brooklyn named Robert Gair?"

"No, honey. I sure didn't," said Grace.

I did. I had heard the story many times. And Mr. Gair had invented it…

"*… by accident!*"

Grace smiled. "You certainly are knowledgeable about your boxes."

"Well, they're just so great. Think of all the ways they help us…."

Grace began serving the pie, possibly in the futile hope of getting off the subject.

"We pack our belongings in them. Our clothing, our dishes, our books. We pack our lives in them and carry them around. Without boxes, we would lose our identities. And people live in them! I mean, it's nothing I'd like to try, but people do live in them." He turned to me. "Maybe we could try that out."

"Being homeless?" I said.

"No. Of course not, silly. But maybe we could spend a night in a cardboard box on the front lawn."

"I don't think I'd like that."

Curtis turned back to Grace. "This one. He just doesn't get it. There's a whole culture to boxes. There's even a museum in France, and one day I'm going to visit there. Why, I bet William Shakespeare would have written a sonnet about boxes if they had existed when he was alive."

"Poxes," I said.

"What?"

I grinned, feeling clever. "Poxes on your boxes."

He didn't get it. "I guess," he replied.

The box conversation dwindled from there, and Curtis inhaled his pie. When I looked over at Grace, I saw the same glazed look in her eyes that Janey had when Curtis was speaking. She was either stroking out or bored senseless. Thank God Curtis didn't see it. No one wants to break a puppy's heart.

About half an hour later we were at the door, taking our leave and thanking Grace for her hospitality. Strangely enough, she looked to have gotten a second wind just as we left. Curtis promised once again to bring her some strong, dependable boxes, and we walked next door to my house. The evening sky rumbled and a few drops of rain darkened Curtis' khakis. I had been expecting a little bedroom play, but he kissed me rather shyly and said good night in the driveway. At the first sign of inclement weather, Curtis always headed for home. Curtis hated driving in the rain.

Twenty minutes later I was sitting in the living room on the sofa with the television on mute as I scanned through the channels. Feed the Cat was sprawled on the floor in the center of the room like she owned the place. The rain was beginning to fall hard and heavy outside, causing the satellite to occasionally lose signal. My attention was scattershot anyway, so I didn't truly mind.

There was a knocking at the door. Not frantic or hurried or resembling anything in films where strangers come knocking in thunderstorms, but strong, so as to be heard above the heavy rain. I opened the door to find Mr. Brock Kimble, soaked and smiling. If this was the closest I would ever come to seeing him in a shower, I decided it was good enough.

He handed me the folder containing my notes. "Sorry I got them wet," he said. His long lashes dripped with small raindrops.

"Thank you! Come in. Get out of the rain. Would you like something to drink?"

"I'm fine." He spoke above the downpour, yet still refused to seek shelter from it. He was a trooper. A storm trooper. The side door had but a stoop to stand on and something hardly sufficient to be called a roof. "Why don't you come out?" he said.

I had to have given him a look of supreme perplexity, because he laughed. I stuck my head out the door and looked around, then looked back at him.

He shrugged and raised his eyebrows in a why-not manner. I put my notes down and grabbed an umbrella.

"Why don't I come out?" I said.

I opened the umbrella on the stoop but had not counted on the wind. Random gusts like brat squalls are common in river valleys. My umbrella was ripped from my grasp and went rolling toward the street.

"Whoa!" Brock yelled in surprise.

Brock chased after the umbrella and, honestly, I chased after Brock. As the umbrella ambled and circled over the soggy lawn, both Brock and I took some ferocious spills. I'm certain we looked as silly as drunk. It was as if the umbrella had a mind of its own. It was free and had no intention of returning to me or the house.

We ran into each other at least three times in our—let's face it—pointless pursuit. (It was only an umbrella, after all.) With each collision I felt a stronger tingle, a charge, as we laughed and touched and locked eyes. Something that would have been an annoying task—chasing about a wheeling and mischievous umbrella—was suddenly and almost embarrassingly as endearing and romantic a scene as I had ever been involved in. Certainly this was nothing I'd ever put into a book. Things like this didn't happen. Not really. When he smacked my ass and shouted "Get 'er!" while grinning something wicked as the umbrella rolled past, my knees nearly gave out.

In the end, Brock gained enough footing to wrangle in the beast. I sat where I had fallen, breathless, beneath a tree, caked in as much mud as he and finding it just as humorous. He offered his hand to help me up, then raised the umbrella above us—as if that was now of any use at all.

"I think," I said over the rain and through my laughter, "a walk may not have been a good idea after all. It appears I was overcome by the moment."

"It *was* a good idea. The umbrella was the saboteur."

And then there was a moment, something I had never experienced with Curtis before, or with anyone for that matter. It was as if everything under was coming out. Blooming. Lids off. Fresh air. I had never been more soaked to the bone, yet as I looked into Brock's eyes, any discomfort left me and all those film clichés suddenly made sense. We said nothing. We stood under the ruined umbrella and I think we would have even kissed if, at that moment, Mrs. Allenson hadn't come out of her house— under a perfectly fine umbrella, thank you—and inquired of me:

"Are you okay, Logan? Is this one of those Mormons? Do you want me to call the fuzz?" She, of course, had been watching us.

I reluctantly broke my gaze from Brock. "No, Grace. We're fine."

"What?" The poor dear couldn't hear over the rain.

"He's a friend," I shouted. "We're... uh, we're just having a bit of fun."

"Oh! Well, that's nice then. Get your play in." She said something about Curtis that I couldn't make out and then she walked back into her house.

"Neighborhood watch?" asked Brock.

"Don't let her fool you. She's a bulldog."

"Why don't I give you a call sometime?" Brock said. "A real call. Not work-related."

"That would be... (not part of my routine) nice."

"Yes. I know." He walked to his car, leaving me in the yard under the umbrella, and he gave me an interested and gorgeous smile as he got in. I was still in the yard over a minute after he had driven away.

great expectations

THERE was a lovely fountain in downtown Adbury, not far from where I lived. Gorgeous nymphs and full-faced angels carved from limestone played frisky and flirtatious games in the water. Moss and wisteria clung to the structure, shading it a gentle green. It was a very romantic fountain, not so large as to be imposing, situated in a small park of well-groomed trees that offered luxurious shade to visitors in the spring and summer and a great dose of aching, colored nostalgia in the autumn. During the winter months, when the water was shut off, the fountain was the centerpiece of holiday festivities, draped in blue and white lights.

Along a stone walkway that circled the fountain there were benches with graceful latticework that reclined in such a way as to be eternally at ease. Brock and I sat on one of these as we enjoyed the summer's day. A light mist from the fountain touched us as we discussed, only at first, my indecisive new literary adventure. It was at least more coherent now, which was saying quite a bit. Since the night of the storm and its umbrella pursuit, I had found a new creative wind. The idea of a spoof had been left far behind, and I now looked on it with embarrassment and a bit of shame. Also, I had a title now: *The Gods Have Jealous Eyes.*

We had stopped by one of the many shops in Adbury that specialize in sweets and confections. I had a coffee. Brock had a monstrous and indulgent-looking ice cream on a huge waffle cone.

It was one of those ice creams kids are awarded with when they do something especially good or obedient. There was every color one could imagine on the thing. There were sprinkles and clumps of fudge and nuts and even a couple of gummy bears. I was amazed that, aside from the initial looks of delight when it was handed to him, Brock was able to eat it with a straight face.

"I like what you're doing with the book," he said, as his ice cream disappeared magically before my eyes. "A sweeping romance beats a spoof any day. And that's a good title. Very Jacqueline Susann."

"Why is that? Comedies still sell well, don't they? Are we that depressed a society that a comedy won't sell?"

"That depends on who writes them. Augusten Burroughs. Yes. He sells like a muscle-daddy sandwich. But you haven't built your name around writing comedies like that. Not flat-out comedies, anyway. Honestly, it was a little lazy of you… if you don't mind me saying."

"I *do* mind you saying!"

He stopped licking and gobbling for a moment. "Sorry," he said. "I was relieved to see you changed the characters' names too. Flavius and Maximus are much more digestible. This will be a great story. A shipwreck on a deserted island, and they're the lone survivors. Good stuff. It reminds of the books I loved when I was a kid. *Robinson Crusoe* and *Treasure Island*."

"Well, there is a third survivor. Septimius or Caligula or something."

"Oh, yeah. The crazy guy. What are you going to do with him?"

"I'm not sure yet. This story is kind of writing itself."

"Will there be sex?"

"Sure. There is always sex."

"Good. Your readers love that. You've touched a lovely nerve with straight women. They, my friend, are your bread and butter. Do right by them and you will have an ever-loyal following."

"They love the gays, huh?"

Brock gave a quick and suggestive lick to his ice cream. "*Love* them!"

I stared straight into him for a moment. I didn't want to stare, but I was not willing to look away. It's not that I couldn't look away. My neck still worked. But he did have an ice cream in his hands. A grown man with an ice cream cone is like a basket full of puppies. Curtis never looked like this. He had his moments of cuteness, but nothing Curtis had ever done had filled me with such protective passion. In fact, the thought of being with Curtis intimately was starting to feel like a job. Some place I deposited sperm once a week. I knew before I had even formed the words in my head that I would need to end things with him. It struck me as a very odd idea. He fit in perfectly, didn't he? He fit into my life perfectly. And at the same time he was wearing a part of me thin. He had become an unwanted groove.

THE town library sat, columned and solemn, on Adbury's Main Street a few blocks down from the fountain. Like many libraries, it had seen its patronage decrease since the advent of the Internet and search engines, but there was still a decent amount of people who thumbed through the racks looking for something they couldn't name. Nothing the Internet can provide can compare to the scent of thousands of old books. Of their aging pages and inks and bindings.

I was at the library with Janey. She was searching the shelves in vain for an obscure title about the Bible and homosexuality, since she couldn't find the book to order from any of her usual Internet stores. She had searched the library's catalogue on the computer and had not fond it there either.

"They have to have it," she said, running her fingers along row after row of book spines as if tickling them. "This is a library. They're supposed to have everything."

"This is Adbury," I said as I searched the opposite shelves. "Not the Library of Congress."

"Well, they have every version of the Bible ever published. That's for goddamn sure! How can anyone need so many versions of the very same book?"

"I don't believe it *is* the same book. Not after thousands of years of translating."

"True. It was probably a cookbook at the very beginning. Then someone adds in their aunt's recipe for beef stew and it all goes to hell."

I was becoming bored, not truly concentrating on the task Janey had given me, and so I started to pick up books that looked interesting, glancing breezily through them. "Speaking of religious matters. How goes the Door-To-Door War?"

"It's getting nasty. The factions are throwing some very dirty looks across the street when they see one another. The most exciting part was yesterday, when a couple of Mormons and a couple of Jehovah's Witnesses had to pass each other on the sidewalk right in front of our house." She was still hunched over and scanning the shelves. "The air was electric."

"They were right at our house and they didn't ring our bell?"

"No. Should I have shouted for them?"

"I know you wanted to."

"Yes. But about that time Curtis drove up. The poor thing would have been mortified."

Curtis. I had made a decision. I needed to stick with that decision, though I felt less certain of it now.

"What was that?" Janey asked. She had stopped molesting the book spines and was now looking at me somewhat suspiciously.

"What?"

"You made a noise."

"Did I?" I put the book I was leafing through back on the shelf. "I'm thinking about breaking it off with Curtis."

Janey's expression was none too subtle. Her eyes might as well have been mirror balls of light. "Excellent!" she exclaimed. "I think that is excellent."

"Hush," I chided her. "This is a library."

"A useless one. I'm going to go ask a librarian where that damn book is." She grabbed my hand as she passed my way. "Excellent!" she said again. "I'm so proud."

The librarian was a young lady with severe black hair cut in a style as straight-formed and as sharp as blades. She did not smile. She did not frown. She studied. Some would say she had the look of a judge. She seemed to take in everything around her, ready to weigh judgment in due course. Despite her rather dull choice in fashion (a solid gray dress with black buttons lined down the front), I imagined she had an interesting life. Maybe she was a stripper on the weekends. Maybe she was a superspy at night. But then, I couldn't have her secret life be more exciting than my own Walter Mitty adventures, could I? In the end, I decided she was indeed only a librarian.

"Can I help you?" she asked, clearly not interested in actually helping us. She didn't blink. She was a vampire. I was sure of it. A vampire with a fanged vagina.

"Yes," Janey said. "I'm looking for the book *Jonathan Loved David* by Tom Horner, but I can't seem to find it. I was wondering if—"

"No. We don't have that book."

"Are you sure? You haven't even looked yet."

"Is it in the computer?" the librarian said knowingly, with a hint of impatience.

Janey rolled her fingernails on the desk. "No, but—"

"Then we don't have it. We don't carry books like *that* anyway." She looked me over. She knew exactly who I was and exactly what kind of books I wrote. I had a modicum of fame in town, but it had never amounted to dinner invitations or pleas for my autograph and I had never once been interviewed by the town paper.

"You don't carry his books either?" Janey asked, gesturing to me.

"Please keep your voice down, ma'am. And no, we don't. Not since last week. We have new guidelines and per these guidelines we have… *cleansed* our shelves of books written by that type."

I rolled my eyes at her. Janey went further.

"Fascist!" she said. She grabbed a book cart and began wheeling it around the stacks, piling on book after book until she disappeared from view. I looked at the librarian and gave as heartfelt a smile as I could dig up. I had no idea what Janey was doing, but she was angry and I knew to stay out of her way when she got like this. She had decimated whole villages in this mood. When at last she returned to the desk with a cart piled high and heavy with books, the librarian at last showed some sort of unrestrained emotion.

"What are you doing?" she demanded.

"I want them all," Janey said.

"All of these? You can't read all of these in two weeks. You can only check books out two weeks at a time, ma'am!"

Janey arched her brow. "I said I want all of these. I'm a speed reader, you little cunt."

The librarian stood, motionless and flustered. People were staring.

"*Every one of them*," said Janey. "You won't be needing them after all, if you have those new guidelines. You see, every one of these writers is a bigger 'mo than my friend here."

In the cart lay the plays of Tennessee Williams, works by Gertrude Stein, Jean Genet, James Baldwin, Walt Whitman, and Gore Vidal, among many others. Among many, many, many others.

"I'm waiting!" Janey snapped at the woman.

I thought to myself, *Sweet baby Jebus! We're going to have a rumble.*

As we left (and thank God not in a police cruiser), Janey pushed the book cart to the car with a victory smile.

"They're just going to get rid of all of those books when you take them back," I said. "It's a war in there."

"Who said a thing about taking them back? I just went shopping, bitch! This will hold me over until Christmas."

Pulling up to the house, back from our library excursion/confrontation, we saw a car in the driveway. I immediately recognized the youthful green of the Volkswagen as that of my mother, Lucille's. She had purchased the car instead of something a bit more sensible because she liked the look of it. It was, as she put it, as playful-looking as a fuzzy tennis ball. I reminded her that it might be tossed around just as easily too. She had given me an *ooooh* brush-off, and when I asked her what Dad thought of it, she big-eyed the response, "He'll learn to love it." That was not so. He could barely fit in it.

"What's your mom doing here?" Janey asked as we got out of the car.

Lucille had been sitting on the front porch swing when we drove up, but now made her way toward us, looking too dressed up for a spontaneous visit. She wore a summery dress of pale blue that was cut above her knees, sharp white heels, and a knockoff purse that hung like jewelry from her forearm. Her blonde hair was done up nice, not a hair out of place, and had recently been highlighted.

"Lucille, what are you doing here?" I asked as she gave me a kiss on the cheek.

"We had plans today," she said cheerfully. "Hey there, Janey!"

"Hi, Lucille."

"Where have you been?" she said to me. "You could have at least left the door unlocked so I wouldn't have had to wait out here on the porch. I hope nobody saw me lurking around the house like some common criminal." She looked around, still smiling so that anyone who was watching would see she was not a supervillain.

"We had plans last week, Lucille. Not this week."

Her smile dropped. "No. Surely not. I had it written on my calendar." She went searching through her purse and found her cell phone/organizer. She waggled it giddily. "I just got it. It's *so* handy. Now, let's see…." She pushed some buttons and made a few comments that were directed at either herself or the organizer until she figured out exactly how to make it do what she wanted. I looked to Janey, who gave me a commiserating smile.

"Aha!" she squealed. "See. Here it… oh, honey. You were right. You certainly were. It *was* last week that we were meant to get together." She slumped. "And I missed it. How could I have forgotten?"

"Well, you're here now," I said, trying not to sound exasperated.

"That's right!" She gave me a tap on the arm. "I sure am. What should we do?"

We ended up in the garden. I made some lemonade and brought a tray of cookies out, not because any of us wanted them, but because that's what one does on summer days. Cookies and lemonade. Lucille took her heels off and helped me pull weeds. Feed the Cat circled her legs and Lucille encouraged the cat's affection with baby talk.

"Who's a sweet little kitty cat? Who is it?"

"Is that Lucy I hear?" Grace was working in her back garden as well. She leaned over the white picket fence, taking off her John Deere hat to wipe away the sweat from her forehead, and waved.

"Hi there, Grace!" Lucille chirped. "Would you like a cookie?"

Grace looked over to the tray sitting on the birdbath. "What kind you got?"

"Well, there's some chocolate chip and some sugar cookies and some of those lemony things the Girls Scouts sell."

"I'll have one of those."

Lucille returned with the tray of cookies and peered over the fence at Grace's own garden. "Looks real good this year."

"Why, thank ya! It's been a good season, especially for my tomatoes. I got the juiciest tomatoes on East Second Street."

Another car pulled into the drive, this one much nicer than the others. I recognized it immediately as Brock's, and suddenly my worlds were colliding. Chaos ruled as he got out of the car, spotted me, and waved.

"Who's the guy in the suit?" Grace wondered aloud. Then, and with a wry smile my way, "Ah. I remember."

I had never expected Grace to be as accepting as she was of my life. A woman from an older generation who had grown up in a small Midwest community and had remained there all of her days didn't exactly say *tolerant* to me when I had first met her. But once I got to know her, I realized the woman would have been the Grand Marshall of the Adbury Gay Pride Parade, if it existed. I was certain Janey had it in mind to tell Grace about our excitement in the library, and I was also certain that soon after that Grace would make known her displeasure with them with a strongly worded visit.

I felt somewhat conspicuous as I sauntered—for surely it was a saunter—over to meet Brock. I had the urge to run at him screaming *Mine! Mine! Mine!* but I controlled myself.

"Looks like a garden party," he said, full-voiced and confident. He carried a package in his hand but did not, at first, address it.

"Brock, this is my mother Lucille, my best friend Janey, and my neighbor Grace. Everyone, this is my editor, Brock Kimble."

My mother caught it, that gleam in my eye and pitch in my voice. Women are always so much better at picking out those notes. Mothers especially. She offered her hand to Brock. "How do you do?" she said, all whites (she had been using a teeth-bleaching agent of late).

"Are those cookies?" Brock asked, eyeing the plate in her hand.

"They sure are! Would you like one?"

"He would," I said.

Brock grabbed a chocolate chip cookie.

"So, are you two dating?" Lucille inquired, her mind suddenly set to "gossip." "What about Curtis? Are you broken up with Curtis? Did you have a fight? What did you fight about?"

Janey stepped up. "Lucille, I have some books in the car. Would you help me bring them into the house?"

"Um... sure, honey...."

As Janey escorted Lucille—with a bit of force—out of the garden I could still plainly hear my mother: "Is he cheating on Curtis? Oh my word! That poor boy. Give me all the dirt...."

Grace was cackling as she leaned on the fence, shaking her head. "That woman!"

"Sorry about that," I said to Brock.

"Don't be. She's sweet. Mother's are supposed to be... sweet." As he spoke, I noticed a brief tick in his words. As if he had missed a beat or had lost his train of thought for a second. "Anyway," he continued, "I just stopped by to bring you this hard copy of all of the notes I've taken so far on your new work."

I took the package from him. "You didn't need to do that. You could have just e-mailed them to me. I'm not *that* high maintenance."

A little bit of air escaped from Grace's mouth.

"It's no big thing. I think it's always good to have a hard copy of notes. Besides, I was in the mood for a drive."

"Well, thank you. I appreciate it."

We stared at one another for a long enough time that Grace, who still stood at the fence, said to Brock, "Would you like some of my tomatoes?"

"Excuse me?" Brock said.

"I got some big, juicy tomatoes this year. I can't eat them all. Would you like some?"

"Do you have some yellows? I love yellow tomatoes."

"*Do I have some yellows?*" Grace said as if it were a silly question. "What kind of garden would this be if I didn't have any yellows? No offense, Logan."

My garden had no yellows. "None taken," I said.

"Those are the best kind to eat raw. Salt 'em up and that's a fucking midday treat. Get on over here and pick you some. C'mon!"

As he hopped over the fence in his Armani suit, Grace gave me an arched eyebrow and leaned over to my side. "So, when are you planning to dump the other one?"

"I'm… I'm not. Well… maybe…."

"It's no good to keep something hanging on the vine after it's done dead, sweetie."

Brock was already biting into a large yellow tomato as he stood in the center of Grace's garden. "Do you have any salt?" he asked.

Sweet baby Jebus!

I DIDN'T want to break up with Curtis in my house, or in his, for that matter. I had only actually even been to his house—a run-of-the-mill ranch home in a subdivision—but a handful of times. I imagined there would be some kind of hushed begging or whimpering on his part to get me to stay with him. I had never seen him get that emotionally distraught before, but my writer's imagination colored the scene with pyrotechnic dramatics. It's not that I thought I was the most wonderful rack of lamb in the oven. I am all too aware of my faults. It's just… he had always shown nothing but adoration toward me. There would be fireworks when I broke it off, I was certain. I wanted to do the deed someplace neutral, so I offered to take him to lunch at a nice eatery in town. There, surrounded by people, a scene of weeping hysterics would be impossible. Curtis hated scenes. He was embarrassed when he dropped a fork.

I went to pick him up at the Little Boxes Big Store. As was usually the case, my eyes glazed over upon entering. Cardboard hanging on the walls, full boxes sitting on display on shelves like they were shoes, tiny boxes behind glass as if they were jewelry. Fascinating. I could only imagine the excitement I would feel if I ever entered the French museum of boxes Curtis had spoken of at Grace's dinner. I was dusted with the scent of stale gifts as I made my way to the back, where he stood by the register. He smiled, but only halfheartedly. He seemed nervous and fidgeted with his glasses, then brushed his hair away from his ears. Was it possible he knew what I was about to do?

"Ready for lunch?" I asked, trying to put on as pleasant an expression as I could muster.

"About that. Listen, we need to talk."

"What's wrong?" *He knew!*

"I've been thinking about this all night, and I think the best way to go about it would be to just get it over with. Just to tell you straight up."

I felt as if my plan had been compromised. Someone was pulling the rug out from under my feet.

"I got a call last night from the bigwigs at corporate. They love what I've been doing. They love my ideas and my passion. They offered me a promotion. They want me to travel and help with sales all over the world."

"Worldwide box sales?"

"I know! Exciting, huh? I can hardly believe it either. This would mean, of course, I would have to spend a lot of time away from here. Away from you. I was even thinking of selling the house. And it wouldn't be fair to you if I just up and left while you were still tied down here—"

"Are you breaking up with me?" Rug pulled.

"I had thought about asking you to come along. I mean, you're a writer, so you have no ties, and maybe the travel experience would be good for you. But I know how much you like your routine."

"Routines can change." What was I doing? Was I trying to get him to take me with him after all? I felt a lump in my throat, but couldn't for all I was worth discern why. This was what I had come here for, after all.

He smiled sweetly. "No. That wouldn't be good for you." He put his hand on my shoulder and adjusted his glasses again. "No scene, babe. No scene. Just give me a kiss and walk away."

I couldn't believe it. Somewhere a mischievous bitch-goddess was laughing at me. A muse of boxes.

I did as he asked. I leaned in and kissed him on the cheek like a good ex, and then walked away. Walked right out of the store, feeling like one of those turntables some of the boxes were displayed on. I wasn't heartbroken. Neither was he. I felt like I had just lost a comfortable shirt. But I did not deny that I liked that shirt. Curtis was part of my routine and now he was just... gone.

I looked back at the storefront once I was outside, trying to digest everything. But that was impossible at the moment, so I got into my car, and as I looked in the mirror, I noticed a bewildered smile. How long had that been there? And one more thing:

Now what?

IT WAS two days later that Brock called me. It was unexpected because most of our conversations were online or via text. Hearing the playfulness in his voice made me a bit giddier than was appropriate for the middle of the day. He just happened to be in Adbury for the day and wanted to know if I'd like to go hiking with him.

"Those hills above Adbury call to me, Logan. They sing to me. There have to be trails through them."

"All kinds of trails," I told him. "The town has designated the park a Place of Interest for tourists like you."

"Well, that was nice of them. I'll come pick you up. How's about it? Slap on your manliest boots and your flanneliest flannel."

"It might be too warm a day for flannel."

"Then come naked."

It was a nice day for a hike. Surprisingly, there weren't too many others taking advantage of the beautiful weather. It was getting late in the season, however. The last of August and school had already started again, so there were no difficult little children for us or nature to contend with. There was a tangible expectation of change in the air. A cool wisp that gave the day an edge. Perfect days are boring when there isn't the occasional chill in the air to remind you of their perfection.

We chose a trail that went steeply uphill, through the trees, and, at the top, offered a wide view of Adbury out to the river and the hills beyond. Everything was still green. Dark green, as if the trees were holding their breath and would suddenly exhale in a burst of autumn color. Brock walked with a branch he had found near the bottom of the trail. "In preparation for my golden years," he said.

He wore a pair of dark-blue mesh shorts and a jersey, exposing the body I'd been sure he had. Toned, tanned, and even. Seen to in every way. How did he find the time, I wondered.

I had dressed in a pair of khaki shorts I thought might catch his eye, and a comfortable T-shirt. I intentionally fell behind as we climbed the trail so I could watch the fabric of his shorts stretch across his great sculpture of ass. His legs showed proof that he was a sportsman. The calves were great balls of muscle and the hamstrings were muscular supports to his behind.

Buttresses. He must have felt me admiring his artwork, because at last he gave me a sly look back over his shoulder.

"My first time with a guy was on a trail in the woods," he said. Not that the mention of sex was completely out of the blue. I had been silently prodding it along, after all.

I caught up with him. "Do tell."

"The whole incident started in school, actually. I was picked on by the straight bullies. One in particular. Terry Gomez. He was one of these big, hulking bad boys who took out their own failings on those around them. If you were different in any way, he picked up on it. I had been a target of his since grade school. He made things miserable for me. One day, in between classes, I passed him in the hallway. My nerves always spiked when I had to pass any of the bullies. Man, I had some killer stomachaches in school. I'm surprised I never had an ulcer. And in those days, bullying was just considered part of growing up.

"Anyway, I passed Terry in the hallway and he called me a fag. Well, for some reason, I'd had it. I don't know why, after years of the taunts and name-calling, I chose that particular episode to react to, but I did. I turned right around and started whaling on him. Just *whaling*. Cursing and fists a-flying. Eventually I was pulled off him and we were sent to the principal's office." Brock laughed. "We had this real ugly-looking principal. Like Hitler-ugly. Weird 'stache and all. He seemed to be on my side. Terry was a known troublemaker after all. But then he said to Terry, 'How would you like it if someone called you gay?' It was an awkward turning point for me. At that point I realized the principal was a bigger jerk than Terry, because by saying that he was implying that being gay was somehow less. As someone older, I thought he would have known better, or at the very least tried to hide his bigotry.

"The next day, having been kicked out of school for the day to think about my actions, I went to the local state park. I've always liked hiking. It clears the head. I had no intention of actually thinking about anything. But who do you think I saw there? Terry Gomez. He was standing right in my path, just staring me down. I thought we were going to get in another fight. I thought he was going to kill me. I mean, he was big and mean and damn, did he look pissed! But instead...."

Brock looked at me and winked.

"Really?" I asked. "In the park?"

"Yep. It was awkward and fumbling, but after that Terry never bullied me again. We never became friends or anything, but that was the end of the abuse."

His eyes were an open door. He took me by the hand and led me off the path behind a tree.

"What are we doing?" I said in light protest. "We can't. This is a public park."

He hushed me. "There's no one around," he said.

The sweet expectation of a kiss was held just a little longer as we stared into each other's eyes, coming so close I could feel the brush of his breath. Where to begin... what to do. I grabbed at his jersey, ready to rip it from him. Ready to sink my teeth into his chest. But first the kiss. It was not long and epic. It was ferocious and starved. He bit my lip and I bit back and with every groan I knew he wanted what I wanted. This would not be the dull, paint-by-numbers interaction I was used to with Curtis. This would be fucking, even if we never had actual sex.

I was petrified. This was against the rules. Against the routine. People were arrested for this kind of thing. If they were found out. And that made it all the more interesting.

With my thumbs, I quickly pulled down his shorts and felt a thick tumble against my thigh. While we kissed, I grabbed his cock, the hot, smooth skin burning my palm. He released my own hardening cock from its confinement, and the two proud things pressed against each another in an intimate introduction. They rolled over and past each other in a lusty dance; they embraced glans to glans. They could not embrace hard enough, it seemed. They kissed sweetly with silver tongues.

My hands tended to other matters, kneading Brock's backside to relaxation, being a gracious guest, and wanting to be asked to enter rather than intruding. I could feel him loosening. I could sense him opening up.

I entered him with somewhat more ease than I had thought it would take, and he rode and grunted and grimaced, acting the part of the pursued and the caught. We were animals fucking in the wild. Just as God had intended. The landscape around me disappeared and there was only Brock. The twigs and small pebbles we lay on and rolled over pinched us and caused a lovely discomfort. When I flipped him over and he lay on his stomach, I felt for the first time that this was how it should be. This exhilaration, this naughty feeling of racing toward something, wind in my hair, solidity below. It reminded me of the first time I had orgasmed, lying on my best friend's back, quite clothed, and roaring down a snow-covered hill on a sled in the middle of winter.

This was beautiful and unexpected and not part of my routine. This was magic.

vanity fair

SWEPT away by an unusual destiny in the blue sea of August. And so I was. And the proof of it was in my writing. My manuscript, my big, sweeping romance titled *The Gods Have Jealous Eyes* was robust and passionate. I imagined a musical score of such fine orchestration to accompany it that even the most cynical and hard-hearted of critics would weep. I was deep into Brock. As deep as anyone could be. Anyone I knew, anyway. I wrote it all for him, to him, and about him. We were the two heroes on the beach, rolling in the sand and the tide. Flavius and Maximus making love beneath an ancient, uncharted sky. A sky full of stars we felt safe naming and cataloging from a distance. Stars that would burn us up in a fraction of a second if we got too close. Stars that pulled at the very tides that swept us up and away.

I was too far in it to feel embarrassed by the things I wrote down.

The third character—the crazy one whom I had imagined as a dethroned emperor the likes of a Commodus or a Caligula—had completely vanished from the story for the time being. I would find use for him later, but I needed to delve deeper into this passion between my leads. I wanted the readers to feel every grain of sand on their skin as they rolled in their growing lovers' embrace. I wanted the readers to taste each kiss.

This newness of passion left me a bit bewildered. At night, I would stare up into the dark of my room and the tedium of my everyday life would once again begin to sink in. Without Curtis to provide some sort of distraction, my lifeless walls were never more evident. And yet he had never provided color to them at all. Just vague movement. It was Brock who had shaken me. Who had set fire to my lists and my routines. But now, what was I to do without them? They anchored me, these lists. And what if Brock and I never touched in an intimate manner ever again? What if our rule-breaking in the hills around Adbury had been a one-time thing? I would be a man without color or purpose or love. Or passion. Most of all passion. For now that I had found it, I never wanted to be without it.

A COUPLE of days passed, and we used every means we had—phone, chat, text, and e-mail—to flirt. I was relieved to see Brock did not view me as the one-time fling I had feared he would. In the course of our daily online discussions about my new book (he was still my editor, after all), Brock asked if I would like to visit him some weekend and stay overnight. Though he might have meant in the weeks ahead, the moment he proposed the idea I already had my sights set on the coming weekend.

"Sure!" he wrote back. "This weekend would be great." And he even crowned the statement with a very cheerful emoticon.

I bounded down the stairs to tell Janey, who sat in perfect poise at the kitchen table, reading a copy of the Bible. Her outfit was unique for her. She had her hair high in a ponytail and wore retro '60s glasses I hadn't seen her wear since college (which explained her squinting, since the prescription probably needed an update). From somewhere deep in her closet she had pulled out a plain white blouse, a boring black skirt, and black, churchy shoes. Her legs were crossed at the ankles.

"What's going on here?" I inquired, the excitement I felt from my newly minted weekend plans stumbling just a bit as I saw her. "Have you converted without them?"

"It's all part of my clever new strategy," she said. "I'm going to look as pious as them. More pious even. They'll feel more comfortable talking to me if they think there's more of a chance they'll fill their quota."

"You look like a naughty schoolgirl, sweetie. You'll give them holy boners."

"I look demure, dammit!" She slammed the Bible on the table. Feed the Cat, who had been watching us from the doorway, skittered to the living room. Janey leaned back in the chair, taking me in. "What's up with you? You seem… happy."

"I'm headed out for the weekend, dearest." I came and sat across from her at the table. "I'm heading to see Brock."

"*Really?*" she said in a drawn-out spoof of the word. "So soon after Curtis?"

"Is it that soon? I haven't thought about that. But it's not like I'm going up there to plan a wedding."

"It's a bit unlike you. That's all I'm saying. You've never been one for sudden changes. Everything is always so planned."

"I'm trying to be more spontaneous, I guess."

Her eyes were large and dissecting beneath the glasses. "So, what exactly are you and Brock? To each other, I mean."

I had to think on this. I had never been in this situation before. Everything and everyone I knew had a nice, neat label. Things and people wore invisible tags.

"I don't know," I said.

"And you're okay with that uncertainty?" she said in her most analytical manner.

"I don't know. I guess I have to be. I don't think I'm too bothered by it."

"Well, you can't lie to yourself. You have to be honest."

I gave her a look up and down. "Is that what they teach you at church? Oh, wait. You've never been to church."

"Slut. Don't change the subject. This isn't about my sins, it's about yours. And you're gay, so according to the Jehovah's Witnesses, yours are already much worse than mine."

I MET Brock's best friend, a straight joker named Bo Penn, that weekend. I remember thinking to myself that it sounded like a made-up name, Bo Penn. Like the bad boy in some film about teenagers, hot-rodding, and rebellion. But then, Logan Brandish didn't exactly sound true to life either.

After my initial arrival at Brock's high-rise apartment in the city (very nice and pretty much on the nose as to what I had expected, with classy fine-lined furnishings and tasteful works of art), Brock and I had some more toe-curling sex. In fact, we got right to it. No sooner had I entered the apartment than my clothes were littered on the floor along with my bag. There were times during that weekend I wondered where on earth all the sexual energy I was expending had been hiding all these years. I was like a gun. He touched me and I went off. If he even looked at me I was half-cocked. I was in a constant state of expectant flush, my flesh warm and tingling.

Bo knocked on the door after we were both spent from exhaustion and could do no more to each other. Bo was a wide guy, in the football player sense of the word. He wasn't overweight, but he was sloppy in the upkeep of his body. It was threatening him: *"One more weekend of pizza and beer, and I quit!"* He had that cocky air about him that many straight men have who've never experienced true rejection. His kind was a dime a dozen in my life. Any gay man in the Midwest will tell you the same thing: if only we could have that level of unearned, arrogant self-confidence. He strode into the apartment with long, heavy steps, carrying a case of beer as if heading to a party. He smiled pleasantly. He had a handsome face and blond hair.

"Who are you this time?" he asked me as he grabbed my hand to shake it.

"I don't understand," I said.

But Brock quickly distracted him. "This is Logan. I told you about him." He took the beer from Bo.

Bo looked the two of us over. "You two have been fucking like prison bait, haven't you?" He was grinning wildly. "Admit it!" He jabbed Brock in the side. "Admit it! You two is trying to have babies!"

Brock laughed like it was the funniest thing he had ever heard.

I suddenly realized I was not going to have much more than lingering looks the rest of the evening. These two were fast friends. Bros before… well, we all know the rest of that tactless line.

Bo leaned toward me and felt my stomach. "Damn, Brock!" he said. "You screwed him good. He's having twins!"

I couldn't even force a smile.

The moment I realized I truly did not like Bo at all came soon after Brock handed me one of the beers Bo had brought. We were watching ESPN on Brock's massive television. Bo was espousing his view on a game he had seen earlier in the day that had nothing to do with the one being played.

(Before I go further I must tell you a bit more about Brock's body. There is a point to it. I promise. Brock had a very nice chest. Pectoral muscles that drew the eyes. I even offered to go jogging with him just to see them in motion. When he crossed his arms, he had cleavage.)

Bo, on receiving a beer from Brock and still rattling on about some phantom game, reached up with his free hand and began squeezing Brock's chest even as he was drinking and talking. It was the oddest thing. Like an involuntary movement. Neither of them seemed to think anything of it, however. And please understand, dear reader, that when I say "squeezed," I'm talking full-on pawing. This was a firm grasp and a deep massage. It might have been construed as sexual if it didn't remind me so much of being on my grandfather's dairy farm.

Brock must have seen my eyes dilate because he shrugged Bo's hand off.

"We've known each other forever," he said, as if he owed me an explanation.

"Don't worry about it, chief," Bo said. "You don't get the Bo-text. I don't want to fuck him. I'm as straight as they come. Honest. But he's always had such nice titties. No man, gay or straight, can avoid a nice rack. Am I right?"

The awkwardness I felt muted me. There was a moment between Bo and me that felt like a standoff. Neither of us wanted to blink.

"What say we finish these beers and head to the bar?" Brock offered.

The bar in reference was a narrow place off the beaten path and built into that hole in the wall you're always hearing about. It was called Stan's and smelled not unpleasantly like beer and burgers. It was dimly lit, crowded, and very noisy. Unable at first to find a booth or a table, the three of us stood at the bar and wasted quarters on a Meg-Touch quiz machine. We did very well in the areas of entertainment and sports, but politics nearly killed us. I was strongest in the music category (for some odd reason, there was no literary category).

"How do you know all that shit?" Bo asked me. "All that shit about music."

I had no answer for him. I just did. That was how I compartmentalized things. One little detail connected to another and another and so on. Leonard Cohen wrote "Hallelujah," which was covered by Jeff Buckley, who died on an evening swim, et cetera, et cetera.

When at last we did find a table and finally got our drinks, it was still as crowded as when we had arrived, and at this point Brock had found some admirers in the form of two heavily intoxicated young men, hillbillies from the country, who were celebrating one of the two's marriage proposal.

"He's gettin' hitched!" the bigger one said, hugging his buddy around the neck. At which point they both broke into hootin' and hollerin' that might have played well at a county fair, but was conspicuous in a big-city bar.

They stared at Brock's arms, two-fisting drinks, and asked him to flex for them. He complied so that they might leave, but you would have thought they were at a strip joint the way they responded. I was beginning to feel sorry for the poor girl who was going to be brought into this fold.

"All the boys love Brock," Bo said, giving my elbow a nudge as Brock placated the marriage party. "That fella is a man about town. He gets laid more than anyone I've ever known. Gay or straight."

"Really?" I said over the crowd.

"Hell, yeah. I get so jealous sometimes. He has the sex life I want. Well, minus the man-pussy, of course."

"Of course." My heart sank. So, according to Brock's best friend, Brock was exactly the kind of guy I'd thought he was that first day we met in the hotel restaurant. I was just another good time.

"Does he still keep in contact with any of those other guys?" I asked.

"I think so. Yeah. You never know when you're gonna be hard up for pussy, am I right?" He nudged me again, but this time with more force. "Why? Are you looking for something more serious?"

"No. No. Absolutely not."

"Well, that's good." He looked dead serious. The playful ballplayer all but vanished. "Because he don't need nothing serious. Not now. You reading the Bo-text here?"

By this time, the two hillbillies had embarrassed themselves by being a bit too touchy-feely with another man in public and had moved from our table. Their hollering had gotten the attention of some annoyed table neighbors, and name-calling had ensued, then a short scuffle. Brock looked at me with a shrug and a lopsided smile. I tried to smile back, but could not do too good a job of it due to the lump in my throat.

The next day was better. Bo was nowhere in sight and I had Brock to myself. We spent the day in utter laziness, tangled in his bedsheets, watching TV, and making out until the afternoon, when we ordered Chinese. In the back of my head, Bo's words from the previous night echoed. "All the boys love Brock." And he had said it as if he knew that I was just another in that line of boys. Or as if he wanted me to believe I was. But I had seen something in Brock's eyes. I knew I had. Something that told me different than what Bo was threatening.

And I thought to myself, wouldn't it be wonderful if it all worked out that neatly? Like lines on a page. Like a numbered list. Like a gift in a box. Everything I've ever wanted but never knew.

We watched a movie that night instead of heading out. Brock had mentioned a club, but I didn't want to share him again. It was childish of me, I know, but Bo would have done the same if he were in my place. I was there to see Brock, not the nightlife. I tried not to take too much glee in the thought of Bo's expression when I heard Brock tell him over the phone we were staying in.

A strange thing happened, though, while we were watching the movie. My head was leaning back on Brock's shoulder, and as the film ended, I started to cry. I had not cried at a movie in years. Especially something as manipulative as this, a mediocre romantic comedy. I didn't think it was possible for me to cry anymore. I was not a heartless man. There have been films I found touching, but to cry over a film was unheard of for me. Yet there I was. I wiped the first tear away in such a shocked manner I might have been batting at a fly or pesky gnat.

"Are you okay?" Brock asked tenderly, brushing my hair with his fingers.

"Yes," I said. "I suppose so. Let me ask you something. Last night, Bo said…."

"I'm going to stop you right there. Don't listen to anything Bo says. He's wrong ninety percent of the time. He thinks he knows much more than he does."

"Really?"

"Really. Something he said has upset you?"

"No. It was the movie."

"Are you sure?"

"Yeah. It was the movie."

the passion

HOME from my weekend with Brock in the city, I discovered a flagging in my wide-eyed optimism about a possible future relationship with him. The conclusions I had jumped to were now wobbly things, and it was all the worse because of how bad I wanted him. I had wanted things before, but never like this.

My dread was a harassing entity. At first it was a pull in my belly and a "but" at the end of every wonderful thought. Soon that morphed into a gnashing of the teeth, a loss of appetite, and—as days passed with only a modicum of talk between Brock and me about the weekend—very little sleep as well. I was restless, a feeling I had never known with Curtis. It felt very unsafe, and not exhilaratingly so. As if I was on a high wire on my first day under the big top. Needless to say—though I will say it anyway—this affected my writing. I had writer's block. All I could think of were Brock and his cock.

I was rocked by Brock's cock and it was giving me a block. What a shock.

I pounded out page after page on my new book, hitting Delete more often than any other key. You could keep tempo to the Delete key. I wanted to blame everything and everyone else for my lack of inspiration and skill. I composed one hell of an angry letter to the Dell Corporation about how evil their laptop— a machine I had been using for three years—was acting toward me. It was the best thing I had written all week. And though I would never send a letter written in such a mood, it felt good to save it anyway, just in case. Anger, my father had always taught me, was best corked and let to ferment. There were times in my life that I questioned my father's wisdom.

After a time, with hours of getting absolutely no real work done, I became convinced that my laptop had put a curse on me. And it did, in fact, blue-screen once, so there was slight proof of its contempt for me. This blue-screen strike by my laptop did very little damage to the little work I had done that night, but that was not the point. My ladylike demeanor all but vanished, and I beat the keyboard as if I were an obsessed pianist pounding at the keys in a musical rage. I beat the hell out of it. By the time my anger was spent, the U key was missing. I never found it.

I went to bed upset with myself for beating on a computer (when they take over the world, I'm sure my rage will be revenged), upset with myself for getting nothing done, but mostly upset because I seemed to have disappointed Brock. I was not what he needed, though I was certain he was exactly what *I* needed. How I got to sleep, even heavily dosed with sleeping pills, I'll never know.

I awoke two hours later and opened my manuscript file. Inspiration, every writer learns, takes a while to hit, and when it does, even if it wakes you from a deep sleep in the dead of night, you must pay heed. You must drag your ass out of bed and write. By morning, the idea you had the night before could be but a faint memory of scattered genius, if it exists at all. So, groggily and still quite under the effects of my sleeping aid, I began to type.

I could not tell you now what exactly I dreamt. There are only bits and pieces that still cling to the walls of my brain. While I was typing, the dream was more evident, but perhaps that was because I was still half-asleep. Not all of the dream made it into my writing, and even as I wrote, other bits that were not truly part of the dream, but only inspired by it, appeared on the page.

The bits that I remember most clearly, and which did not make it into the manuscript, could have certainly been used some day in something more erotic. There were men. Lots of men, and they were at a fort. I was in their midst, high on a battlement wall. The sky was streaked comic-book blood-red and orange. Most of the background was in silhouette and shadow, but what could be seen was jagged and harsh. The men were, for the most part, naked, wearing only leather belts or shoulder straps for knives and weapons. Some wore thick boots as well. They were muscular and many had beards. All had dark hair and eyes of cold ferocity. It was apparent to me this was a barbaric state and they were in the middle of some great war. Meaty, naked bodies, some hacked and headless, lay all around the fort. Below the wall lay more bodies and across a pitch-black river was a charging horde of other similar men.

I looked behind me and I saw a group of my own men lined in two rows, one behind the other, upon a fort wall higher still. They looked determined and ready for battle. And here is where it got very strange. Every one of the men had raging hard-ons, some of which looked painfully erect and others dribbling precum even as the battle raged. The front line of men pushed their bare asses back onto the second, each of the front line taking into his ass and guts a large, erect, and angry-looking penis. In a thunderous instant, without so much as a pump or thrust, the second line yelled in unison and the first line was sent sailing through the air, fired into the charging barbarians like knife-wielding weapons and followed by streams of brilliant white against the red sky.

Of course, dear reader, that did not make it into my manuscript. What would you think of me if it did?

HE RAISED his eyebrow at me. "What the hell is this?"

Brock had just finished reading my newest alterations and what I believed to be utterly brilliant additions to *The Gods Have Jealous Eyes*. I was ready to be drowned with praise.

"What the Helen Mirren did you do to your book?"

I suddenly felt like a disappointing child in the overstuffed armchair of Brock's office at the publishing house. I had had a fixed smile since I came in, completely confident that what I was giving him was the best I could do. My smile twitched now.

"You don't like it? I slaved all week working on it. I hardly got any sleep. Inspiration hit and—"

"It's very well written, but it's depressing as all hell. How am I supposed to sell this? You've killed off a main character halfway in."

It's true. I had.

"But didn't you think it was well done? There're so many different avenues I can explore now with Maximus out of the way."

"Very well done. Yes. But in the type of book you originally set out to write, the kind that you promised us, it doesn't quite work. You just can't have one romantic lead being manipulated and betrayed by the other like this. Readers will not forgive it. And what's worse, you have the poor bastard dying in an undertow while fishing for supper. He can't catch a break. And Flavius, in the meantime, is waltzing over to the other side of the island with a crazy man."

"A hot crazy man," I interjected, as if it mattered.

~ 67 ~

"A hot crazy man. Yes. The hottest crazy man since Gorgeous McCrazy-butt. Okay? That's not the point…."

"That's not even a real character name," I mumbled.

Brock did not look pleased at all with my stubborn attitude. As I watched him, he had suddenly become a villain in his big office chair. A big Lionel Barrymore-style villain, out to disassemble my literary masterpiece. His eyes fired angry bolts at me. If he had breathed fire, I would not have thought it impossible.

I wanted to have sex with him.

"Logan," he said. He might have even seethed the words. "Rewrite this. Make it lovely and romantic again. That's what everyone wants from you. You're good at it."

"People kill main characters in the middle of books all the time," I protested, though at the moment I couldn't think of an example.

"Not in this type of book. There are templates that must be followed. You're not writing *L.A. Confidential* here." (Ha! See. There's one.) "Kevin Spacey can't be killed off in the middle of your romance."

"Number one: Kevin Spacey wasn't in the book *L.A. Confidential*. His character was. Number Two: I would never write a part for Kevin Spacey in one of my books."

"I'm going to kick your ass if you don't grow up."

I was certain he meant it. I remembered the Terry Gomez story and I shut up. "Fine," I said.

"Good." Brock returned to form. "On to other things then. Are you all set for the book signing this weekend?"

The Verona College Bookstore (Adbury had no bookstore of its own) was hosting the event. I was not a fan of book signings. They went against my hermitlike lifestyle. Writing about people was fine. But actually meeting them? That was painful. Signings always felt akin to waiting to be picked for teams in gym class. They were a show of popularity. Of what people actually thought of you and your work. It was good to know at least three or four people in the vicinity of a signing who you could count on to show up. How well your books sold throughout the year meant nothing when a signing came around. People could love your writing but not give two footnotes about seeing you live and in person.

"I think I'm ready," I said.

"Whore yourself up, babe." He winked. "You're purty. Use that to our advantage."

The meeting was over soon after. He gave me a quick kiss before opening his office door and letting me out into the hallway. "Sorry I had to get mean back there," he said.

As I was leaving, all I could think about was Brock looking mean and overwhelming, looming over his desk like a vengeful Greek god. I should have pushed him further. I wanted him to pound his anger into me. And then I wanted to reciprocate the action. I wanted to reciprocate him so hard we'd need to resuscitate.

JANEY was like a lovely spider. She had spun a web and lured in two of the prettiest Mormon boys I had ever seen. They sat at the kitchen table with her, backs straight, their hair cut neatly, their white shirts gleaming. She was once again dressed just as demurely as she had been days earlier, except now she wore a different set of glasses, with pointed rims, and her hair was swept up in a precious little bun.

I gave her a nod to let her know I was impressed. I had come downstairs to get something to snack on. It was early afternoon and I had been toiling away on the rewrite I had promised Brock. It was a torturous rewrite. More so than usual because, for the first time in a long while, I felt I had written something very good.

"Would your husband care to join us?" one of the sweet things asked Janey as I rummaged through the cabinets.

I heard her chortle (yes, that is a word). "No. Not just yet."

These little Mormons knew perfectly well Janey and I weren't married. It was as if they were simply putting an exclamation to the fact. I suddenly felt as if I had wandered into the middle of a porn shoot. *Latter Day Interruptus.* My friend Cliff had done a film like that.

"I have work to do upstairs," I said, having grabbed what was left of a cold seven-layer salad out of the refrigerator. (At least three layers had been picked clean by Janey.) I turned to head back to my room when Janey called for me in an excited manner.

"I nearly forgot!" she said, raising her hands in dramatic good-girl fashion (no painted nails, either). "Excuse me, won't you," she said to the young men. She rose, straightened her black skirt, and shuffled toward me in her heels.

"Nice," I said, giving a knowing smile.

"I know, right?" Every bit the lovely spider. She eats her men whole after sex. "You should have seen what I had to do to finally get them to come inside. If I had writhed on the ground claiming possession it wouldn't have worked as well as this."

She later told me that, completely fed up with being overlooked by all of God's ministers, she burst onto the front porch as these two young men were passing and shouted verse at them:

Be He of vengeance or mercy, the boy could not tell
God was God, Heaven was Heaven, & Hell was blasted Hell
The angels watched in frozen shock, no use to their God at all
"You're a fuckin' dick!" the boy said, and kicked God in the balls.

I suppose she wrote it herself. The boys, thinking Janey was a woman on the verge of a spiritual breakdown, naturally came to her aid. She even feigned a fainting spell so that they would help her into the house.

"I have a date for you," she said, returning now to the reason she had called me back.

"A date? Janey, I'm not dating right now."

"And that's Brock's fault. He's your undate. You need to get over him. Besides, this guy sounds like fun."

"Sounds? You don't know him either?"

"No. But he comes very highly recommended. He's a coach at Verona College. That could be fun, huh?"

"I don't know, Janey."

"Oh, just give it a try." She gave me a quick shove. I could tell she wanted to give me a playful smack, but she didn't want the Mormons to think she was a violent person.

"Alright. When?"

"Tomorrow night."

"Tomorrow?" My voice shook the room. The boys looked at us in concern.

"We'll talk about it later, hon," she said with a harmless grin and girlied herself back to the table.

I threw the salad into the wastebasket and went back to my work.

THE following evening I met my date at a pricey Italian restaurant in town. A place I would have never normally gone. It shook the walls of my comfort zone. By the circumference of his eyes, it did his as well. I wondered, then, why on earth he would have chosen such a place for a date. If he was looking to impress me, this was not the route to take.

He was already seated at the table. He stood too quickly and extended his hand. "I'm Lenny," he said. I introduced myself. We shook awkwardly. He bobbed a bit before he sat, as if he was still trying to figure out dating etiquette. Then, after I had taken my seat, he finally sat back down.

He was an average-looking man. A bit like Curtis in that respect, only Lenny was showing signs of early baldness. He was dressed like a frat boy at a college formal. Everything about his attire was crumpled and rushed and I noticed a light touch of perspiration on his forehead. He looked at me eagerly, as if waiting for me to say something and get the ball rolling. I had nothing.

"You smell... good," he finally said. "You must have showered before you got here."

"Thank you. I try not to offend too many people," I replied. "So, you work at the college?"

I noticed a smidgeon of relaxation in his demeanor. "Yeah. I'm the assistant coach of the football team."

"And the team is doing well?"

"Yeah. Real good... er, well. We've got a great team this year."

A steady stream of wordless moments passed us by, relieved only by the waitress taking our order. Lenny was fidgeting under the table, bouncing a leg nervously. His leg was making the silverware rattle. We ordered with no conversation between us. The waitress, a young lady from the college, gave me a sympathetic look before she left the table.

"You're a writer," he finally said. "I don't really read. I mean, what's the point after you graduate from school, right?"

"I like to read," I said. It was all I could say to such a thoughtless statement.

We both spent the next ten minutes trying to find something of interest in our surroundings. Something we could turn into conversation. But after a few failed attempts at levity, we both saw it was pointless.

The food was brought to us and the table continued to shake. I tried to urge on conversation about anything—where we had grown up, our education, favorite songs—but we had very little in common, it seemed. It didn't help that Lenny preferred single-word answers to most of my questions. It was as if he wasn't even trying. This was, in actuality, truer than I knew.

Being grown men at a small, fancy restaurant, we were set at a small, fancy restaurant table. There wasn't much in the way of legroom beneath it. Every time my leg would accidentally brush against his, the shaking of the table intensified.

"Are you okay?" I asked, legitimately concerned he was having a seizure when the table began to scoot.

"I'm fine. I'm f-fine." He took a long drink of water. Sweat was beginning to pool on his face.

As I drew my leg back, it brushed against Lenny's again. He jumped up, his face as white and frightened as if I'd held a gun to his genitals. "I'm not gay!" he shouted.

Everyone looked at us. I was completely mortified.

"What?"

"I'm not a gay. So you best just stop flirting right now. You ain't getting none of this. I thought I could do it, but I can't. I ain't a gay."

"What are you talking about? Why did you agree to come out with me if you're not gay?"

Lenny sat down once more, quieting himself sufficiently and hunching over the table as if his words were precious things that were in danger of being heard. "I don't want to hurt your feelings or anything, but…. My friend and me, we were at a bar. He's the coach of the team. He said I would never be able to get a gay guy interested in me. That no gay man would even give me a second look. He didn't say those exact words, but that's what he meant. Well, I took it as a dare. I said to myself, 'Well, hell yeah, I can!' And so I set out to snag me a gay to prove him wrong. It sounded like a good idea when I thought it up."

I put down my fork. "Did it? You went out with me tonight because you wanted to prove you could get a gay man interested in you? Jesus Christ! What would have happened if the night had progressed and I *had* been interested in you—which, by the way,

I am most definitely not? At what point would you have stopped it and said, 'Nope. Just kidding'?"

"I—I didn't think that far ahead." He was still leaning over the table, speaking in a hushed manner.

I looked around me in disbelief at the snickering diners. The waitress looked absolutely enthralled with the show.

"I'm going to kill Janey," I muttered. I threw down my napkin and rose. "I could kick your ass for wasting my time like this," I growled. I turned to leave, then, in a moment befitting my literary design, I turned around and said, "And Lenny? Your friend was right. You could never get a gay."

BROCK had never been to Verona College, so I suggested we meet at my house and take the trip together from there. He was in no danger of getting lost if he drove to the college alone. He had a GPS after all. No, what this came down to was me wanting to be in his company as much as possible. It was only a twenty-minute drive from where I lived to Verona College, but that was twenty *more* minutes.

It was a lovely early September day. School had just begun and the students walked alone or in scattered bunches here and there across the great lawns. The campus was a beautifully tree-lined garden that overlooked the river. Follow that river a small distance and you'd find Adbury. Situated throughout were classrooms and dormitories designed in the Georgian style. In the deep fall, when the leaves turned, this small, somewhat insignificant campus looked majestic and melancholy.

There was no parking near the bookstore, which was located in the basement of the campus center, so we parked at the athletics field and walked. Verona was not a school of exorbitant size, and neither was the walk of exorbitant length. Brock breathed deep, taking in the richness around him. He took my hand and gently squeezed it.

"This is lovely," he said. He held my gaze for a moment as we walked. I thought he was about to say something, but whatever it was, he decided against it and looked away, letting go of my hand.

We heard a motorized vehicle coming up behind us on the road. Something small and wheezing. It was not long before we saw it was a golf cart. It sped up to us, then stopped in a stubborn squeal beside us. The driver was a little blonde woman with a wide face and a tightly pulled ponytail. She wore a yellow sweatshirt that proclaimed "Verona College" and a pair of decades-old blue jeans. She smiled broadly. "You two need a ride?" she asked loudly. "I've got plenty of room."

I was perfectly content to walk the rest of the way to the bookstore with Brock, and was preparing to say "no thank you" when Brock spoke up.

"We would love one!" he said as he leapt into the cart. You would have thought it was a ride at an amusement park. "Thank you. I'm Brock. This is Logan. He's doing a book signing at the campus center today."

I got into the cart behind Brock.

"I'm Coach Katie Hammond," the woman said. "You two ever been in a golf cart?"

"Sure," I said.

"Not one like this, you haven't. Hold on to yer britches!"

With that, the cart sped off, squealing in the direction of the campus center. I held tight to my seat, a bit unnerved by the situation. Brock, however, was clearly enjoying himself. Katie's frenetic driving made him hoot and laugh like a boy, and suddenly the amusement park analogy did not seem so far off.

"Yee-haw!" he hollered. He was even allowed to honk the horn for her on a couple of occasions.

"Some of these professors just bring it on themselves," she said. "It's about respect, you see. If they respect that I'm on the road, they won't get flattened."

"Damn straight!" Brock shouted.

"I like your style, cowboy!" she shouted back.

Brock reached back, his face so filled with joy it made me laugh, and smacked me on the knee. "Yee-haw!"

"Yee-haw!" I replied.

"Yee-haw!" Katie echoed.

Katie kindly pointed out to us the most beloved and most reviled faculty on campus as we raced past them, caring for neither sidewalk nor security. We could tell whom she disliked and how much she disliked them by how fast she drove and how far she went out of her way to flatten them. I was more than mildly amused, but honestly more concerned with staying in the cart. But that changed when I saw Assistant Football Coach Lenny, my non-date from a few nights before, whom Janey was still apologizing for. He was spotted crossing the street in front of the campus center and, without saying a word, I leaned forward and thrust out my index finger.

"Good call, cowboy!" Katie said. "I hate that prick! Let's castrate him. Holler 'Yee-haw', boys!"

"Yee-haw!" we both hollered.

Lenny dove into some nearby bushes to escape the cart, dropping the pan pizza he had just purchased from the restaurant in the campus center basement. I couldn't help but give the air a fist pump.

When Katie dropped us off, our collective energy level was spiked. We thanked her with high fives and laughter.

"I'll be here later on if you want a ride back to your car," she offered.

"Hey, you bet, Lady," Brock said.

Inside the campus center, we went down the marble steps to the bookstore. There was a table set up just outside the doors with copies of my three published books already positioned on it and a big photo of my smiling, fake-baked face. It was not an unattractive photograph, but I remembered what I was thinking when that picture was taken: "Is this good? This smile? Is it too pleading? Or not pleading enough? Wait, I can do better."

The signing, on the whole, went better than I had expected. I really wasn't certain any of the students at Verona College would even be aware of my existence, but I was proven wrong. A few people from Adbury stopped by as well, but the majority were the faculty and student body. My Amazon sales rank, which any writer will tell you becomes an obsessive part of your daily routine once you've been published ("just be above 1,000,000 today, *please!*"), had been dismal of late, and I feared this trend would extend to any signings. Happily, it was not so.

"They all love you," Brock leaned over and whispered after my not-so-flawless reading of a chapter from my third book, *Trouble Trouble Trouble*. His eyes dazzled with pride as he crossed his arms over a puffed chest. The fact that people had stayed for my entire reading was no surprise, given that he was standing behind me the entire time, looking like God's very own centerfold.

But truthfully, I didn't need all of them to love me. I didn't even need *one* of them to love me. I realized I simply wanted him to fall in love with me. That was all. Was I in love with him? I didn't know. There were moments I swore I was. But I hadn't been in love with anyone before so I had nothing to compare these new feelings to. They tell you, "You'll know when it's love." Well, maybe afterward.

ERIC ARVIN

sweet bird of youth

AFTER my signing, I felt encouraged—nay, inspired—to write, words of such elegance and poetry that flowers would blossom. Words of such beauty and grace they would fill out the night sky like stars. This was verse. This was writing. I was saturated in words. Every paragraph was an epic. Maximus was not dead after all, due to some miraculous event (enter a caring island god), and Flavius had not run off with Caligula but had been kidnapped by him. I wrote for my lovers such a reunion on the beach as to make stones weep.

"This is crap," Brock said. "What the hell is wrong with you lately? The style is completely at odds with the style of the rest of the book. Were you drinking? Or were you not drinking enough? If the former, stop. If the latter, down it."

I couldn't believe what I was hearing. After all, the reunion, every beautiful syllable of it, was inspired by Brock. By the look in his eyes at the signing, by the touch of his hand as we walked to the campus center before being picked up by Katie.

"This is what you want, isn't it? He's alive and they're together."

"But what type of book is it, Logan?" He was emphatic. We sat at the kitchen table in my house, a friendlier environment than a large office building. Janey was working. Feed the Cat rubbed up against our legs, purring and making a figure eight as she went from one set of gams to the other.

His question had merit. I had no idea what I was writing. Was it a romance or an adventure? Was it a thriller or a character study? Mythology or history? I didn't know. It just *was*. It was just there and unfolding, uncontrolled on my part. It had no parameters or walls. Nothing to keep it tame within a certain literary genre. But was that such a bad thing?

"It is if you have an already well-defined market expecting a certain type of book. We've discussed this before."

"And if I want to change my market?"

"Do you?"

"Sometimes. Maybe. I never had this urge before. This itch for change. For something different. But in the last few months, since I met you," (there, I said it) "since I started working on this book, I'm not sure what I want. My routines are all thrown off. They don't match up anymore."

I only regretted saying what I had when it was met with silence. Feed the Cat's continuous purring was the loudest thing in the room. The implication of my words, the deep hope behind them, and the quality of restlessness—the weight of it—took the form of a small, pathetic beggar on his knees right there with the salt and pepper shakers in the middle of the table.

"We still haven't seen to the issue we were dealing with the last time we met," he said. "That's all." I was relieved to hear him ignore the beggar, and yet I wanted to cry. "You're in a rut. You need a change of pace. Of surroundings."

"But... maybe you could read some more? Maybe you'll like it more the further you read. I mean, after all, you stopped midway through the new stuff." I became the beggar. "Please."

He looked back to the pages in front of him, his lovely eyes taking in line after line. He cleared his throat.

"O sweet love!" he read. *"The very sinewy arms of pernicious Hell itself could not keep me from you! Our souls are entwined. Our fates are one. O sweet love! Hold me in your arms for all time, even if the very island were to...."* He stopped and looked up at me.

"Well, sure," I conceded. "Anything is going to sound ridiculous if you read it like *that*."

"You're so much better than this, Logan." He rested his elbows over the manuscript. "I have an idea," he said. "Clearly, you need something to inspire you."

"I thought I was pretty damn inspired when I wrote that."

"Well, then you need something else to take you out of your comfort zone, out of your box. I'm heading up north to the family cabin on the lake next week. We're having a gathering. A get-together. It's not really a reunion because, excluding me, they see one another all the time. Why don't you come with me? There will be others besides family there too, so you won't feel like an outsider. I promise."

I have to admit my heart skipped a beat. He was asking me to meet his family. Okay, not in the romantic, husband-to-be kind of way, but one can pretend.

"Are you sure that will be okay with your family?"

"Of course! Our gatherings are always more social parties than family get-togethers anyway. And it will be good for me to have someone else there. You can be my buffer."

Maybe he was right. Maybe a getaway would grease the chain a bit and get things going more smoothly with my writing.

"We can get nekkid." He winked.

I accepted the invite.

THE family's lakeside cabin was four hours north of Adbury. On the drive there, we entertained ourselves with light conversation and music. There would be no talk whatsoever of the book. Brock had decided this at the outset. I was given the task of finding some good music to travel to, i.e., sing along with. In the end, the travel-music catalog had everything from the Traveling Wilburys to Kylie Minogue, from the gay-stereotypical to the unexpected. Anthems were good; ballads were not. One moment we were singing along to the throaty brashness of Neko Case and the next we were bobbing our heads to some pop confectionary who would be forgotten in a year. We were friends on a road trip, and as much fun as I was having trading stanzas with Brock, the thought knifed me in the gut that "friends" was all we were or might ever be.

"Thanks for inviting me along," I said, turning down the volume half an hour into the drive as Madonna sang her confessions. "I should get out of Adbury more."

"I can't believe you live there. It's so small. I mean, it would be a nice place for a weekend getaway, but a home? You seem so Big City to me."

"When I was growing up, I lived out in the country in what was once a little farmhouse. There was never anything to do. I didn't have a lot of friends except for a very select few from school. Still, no one ever came over to play. We lived too far out. I always thought to myself, *When I grow up, I'm going to move to the city*."

"What happened?"

"It just never fit into my plans, I guess. I never really had the opportunity. There was college, of course, but I had decided I wanted to attend a small school by the time I got to that age."

"Sounds like things were locked in at a pretty young age. You set up some boundaries you were unwilling to cross."

"I see that now. You know, to be honest, I really haven't traveled all that much in the past ten years."

"Well, there's your problem!" He said it as if it were so obvious, which I suppose it was to anyone but me. "A writer has to travel. A writer has to get some other experiences. He has to see things that fill him with awe or just plain piss him off. How else do you expect to keep inspired if you don't meet new people or see new things?"

"Imagination."

Brock huffed. "Imagination only gets you so far. Look at *Star Wars*. Besides, you have to *see* something new first—at least a spark of something new—before your imagination takes over and turns it into something great."

It made sense. It was irritatingly simple, but it made sense.

As we continued on, Brock kept referring to the "family log cabin," so I was expecting something quaint and small. I could not fathom how he planned to fit so large a number of people into something already so snug and cozy. The idea of some Laura Ingalls Wilder fantasy cabin, however, was quickly put to everlasting rest when I saw the place. Though it fit quite well into the pine trees, the "family log cabin" was far from quaint. It was a large, three-story structure with long windows facing the lake to let in as much natural light as possible. The second story was wrapped with a porch (where plumes from grilling could already be seen drifting skyward). Out in front was a dock where a small boat was moored. There were also three large canoes leaning up against the side of the cabin in preparation of the family gathering. The party seemed to be well underway when we arrived.

"Do you do a lot of swimming?" I asked, getting out of the car.

Brock gave another huff. "No. But everyone else does. My father was a championship swimmer when he was young." Brock had told me before we left that his father was very ill now, and not the man he had once been. "But let's not talk about that, okay?"

"Okay," I agreed.

"It's just that swimming is a sore subject for me."

We got our bags and went inside.

"We're sharing a room," he said. "Is that okay?"

I gave him a sly look. "What do you think?"

I noticed that, because of the large windows that looked out onto the lake, the inside of the house had a clearheaded feel to it. It encouraged deep, cleansing breaths and, despite all the people, still felt open even while offering that woodsy embrace cabins are known for. I was introduced to Brock's siblings (a brother and two sisters, all older and with budding families), his friends (a couple of colleagues from the publishing industry I was vaguely familiar with), and his mother, a short woman with frizzled golden hair and a perpetually worried expression. He gave her a quick peck on the cheek when he saw her.

"Where's Bo?" I asked him with a playful jab.

"I didn't invite him," he replied with a grin.

"That will save us on alcohol," his brother, Randy, said with a slightly haughty air to his voice.

"How's Dad?" Brock asked his mother.

"He's sleeping, hon," she said. "The meds did him in this morning. He'll be well enough to be out later with us, hopefully."

For a moment Brock's expression nearly matched his mother's.

"He's fine. Don't worry." She patted him on the shoulder; it looked forced. She turned to me. "Logan, it's wonderful to meet you. You are going to have a fantastic time here. I have to go and get some things from the kitchen and take them out to the grill. Uncle Freddy is probably cursing a blue streak right about now. Brock, honey, why don't you two go put your things in your room?"

Brock's room did not face the lake, but instead fronted the trees to the cabin's south side. The room was located high on the third floor, so the trees did not totally block the skyline.

"My room was on the other side of the house when I was younger." The bags were on the bed and we both stood looking out the window. I instinctively wanted to put an arm around him but I didn't.

"And now?"

"And now it's not."

The sounds of a party underway—the warm shouts of familiarity and laughter half-soaked in wine—brought Brock and me out to the wraparound deck on the second floor. As I looked down, even more family and friends sat on the lawn chairs below us, and still others dangled their bare feet off the dock. All ages were represented here and each fitting into its stereotype nicely. Into its box. The fathers grilled the food and drank beers, the mothers gossiped and watched after their younger children, and the teenagers tried their best to separate themselves from the flock.

I followed Brock's lead and mingled with new acquaintances. Everyone was pleasant enough, and I found myself taking mental notes on particular quirks that might make for a good character. I had never been one to start conversations, though, so once Brock left my side to help bring a keg up to the deck, I found myself wandering back into the cabin, not out of boredom, but in interest.

The cabin's walls were lined with photographs, all arranged precisely and framed expertly. Great care had gone into the placement of every hanging. I looked from wall to wall, from table to table and shelf to shelf, briefly scanning some of them, more acutely dissecting others. I noticed in the photos of Brock there was a change. Not a physical transformation, though that was a given, but something more intuitive. Around fifteen or sixteen something had happened, because that's when I noticed the change. His smile was still there, still the same catch trap of beauty, mischief, and sass, but unlike his earlier childhood photographs, there began to evolve a weighted struggle. Almost as if the joy and purity of childhood had become harder to find. Or been taken too early.

There were much older photographs as well, and these were of Brock's father, the man I had yet to meet, in his younger, championship days. He was every bit as handsome as Brock. Older photographs always had the feel to me of untouchable things or falsehoods. As if the people in them could never have truly existed. There seemed to be a sepia veil that separated them from us. As if everything before I developed a consciousness of time was only special effects. Every old photo so unreal as to be a film set staged with fibs.

"That's me after I won the qualifiers for the Olympics."

I was startled by the voice behind me. An old man, feeble and hooked to an oxygen tank, sat on one of the plush sofas. He was so frail and thin a thing I thought it entirely plausible he had been there the whole time.

"Brock is your mirror image," I said, walking toward the man with the photo in my hand.

"He is that. In every way." He reached for the photo. "May I see it?"

I gave it to him and sat beside him on the sofa.

He looked at the picture with such nostalgia and heartbreak I wondered if I should have given it to him. "Glory days," he said. It almost felt as if they were words I was not meant to hear. He looked at me and smiled. There he was. There was Brock, aged decades in a second. "My name's Raymond."

He held out his hand, this time to shake. I took his hand in mine. It was so delicate where once such virility had apparently been.

"I'm Logan." There was no one else in the house at the moment. The party remained outside. Laughter spiked the air.

"You're my son's friend?"

"I am."

"How is he doing these days? How is he *really* doing?"

"He seems to be very well. Very happy. He has a great career and many people who love him."

"Good choice of word. We all *seem* to be different things to get by." He breathed uncomfortably with his apparatus. "I seem to be an old man, don't I? But would you believe that beneath this old skin that same young swimmer from this photograph still exists? Would you believe he has never died? That his wishes and hopes are still as strong?"

"I can believe that," I said quietly.

"We never get old. We just get worn out."

From behind us I heard someone enter the room, though I did not look to see who it was—Raymond's last statement had jarred me.

"I see you've met my father," Brock said to me. He approached and kissed Raymond on the forehead, taking the photograph without saying a word. "He never talks anymore. He just sits there and looks at the old photos. We don't even know if he recognizes what they are."

Somewhat shocked, I looked at Raymond, but his eyes were now downcast and glassed over. He was inanimate, completely closed down.

"I'll let Mom know he's awake. Let's rejoin the party."

I left with Brock, but not before one last look at Raymond to see if I could catch a glimpse of the man I had been talking with. But no. He was gone. I thought about telling Brock what had happened, but really, what would be the point? And besides, that might stir up resentment toward me from Brock, who hadn't spoken to his dad in years.

On the deck, evening was setting in and the music and laughter had increased in volume. After telling his mother about Raymond being awake, Brock devoted his full attention to the party. His dance was an embarrassing yet charming mix of satire and aerobics. His arms flailed as he danced in front of me like some exotic bird during courting season. Those around us watched and laughed affectionately at his baboonery. There were head-shakes and looks that read plainly, "That Brock!" I was uncertain if this dance was an example of his true rhythmic nature or if it was all show. I had a feeling it was the latter, seeing as

Brock was so good at everything else. A man like him would strive to be the best in all aspects of his life just in case it might one day help him get ahead.

"Come on!" he said to me. "Dance like you're nuts."

When he saw I wasn't about to make a fool of myself in front of his family and friends, he danced even more fitfully, driving into a voodoo panic as those around us cheered him on. Only the family dogs, two large and extremely affectionate mastiffs, accepted his dance requests. This wasn't dancing. This was seizing for show.

I was right. He was a showman.

I DON'T remember exactly when I climbed up the stairs to our room. I know it was a while before him, but a while after many others. I was well sloshed, and must have launched onto the bed, falling asleep before I even felt the sheets beneath me.

I woke up sometime during the night, however, and felt the secure grip of Brock's arms around me in a cuddle. This I found satisfying—his heavy, drunken breaths on the back of my neck, the warmth of his flesh—and I quickly fell back asleep. Despite what you may have heard or would assume, sex is not implied every time two gay men sleep together. Sometimes companionship is enough. I had no expectations of intimacy with Brock on this trip, so a cuddle was a delight. And he was a fine cuddler. Tight, silent, and warm.

I woke up again hours later, when morning light was spilling into the room and Brock was already up and gone. I oriented myself to where I was and got dressed. I found him and a small contingent of his family on the deck outside, drinking coffee and eating pastries bought from a nearby bakery.

"You're up!" Brock shouted cheerfully as I walked barefoot onto the deck, still rubbing the sleep from my eyes. I was met by the dogs and gave them the appropriate lovin'.

"Do you want something to eat?" his mother asked. She motioned to the cluttered wood table where the morning buffet was set up. "There's coffee, juice, doughnuts, cereal, and anything else you want. There are also some leftovers from last night I can warm up."

I grabbed a bagel and an orange juice and sat beside Brock. He gave me a clean-eyed smile and patted my knee. Across from us were his mother and Raymond, who was wrapped in an old quilt to keep him warm. Again, I tried to find the man I had spoken with briefly the night before, but all I saw was distance when I looked into his eyes.

"I bring him out every morning," Brock's mother said. She fixed his turned collar. "It seems to give him energy—at least a little more life."

I noticed Brock deflate a little next to me, and it was as if someone had called for a moment of silence over the whole group. Everyone was thinking of something, but nobody was naming the sin. There was, though, a sense of accusation and blame in the looks Randy was flashing at Brock.

Finally, Brock turned to me. "Quite a party, huh? I was impressed you could drink that much. And the singing? Where did that come from?"

"Singing? I don't remember any singing." I looked around for confirmation from everyone else as I chewed on my bagel.

One of Brock's sisters, Jo, started laughing. "You were so funny! I have never heard a man's voice go so *high*."

I cowered in embarrassment, bowing my head and closing my eyes.

Jo continued. "And then to show everyone that your high voice had nothing to do with a deficit of genitalia…."

Her mother picked up the story: "You whipped it out!"

I looked at Brock, horrified. "I didn't!"

He was laughing as hard as the rest of them. "You did. Thank goodness all the children were in their beds."

"Don't worry, sweetie," his mother said. "Brock took good care of you. He made certain you went no further. Got you down off that table like a shocked boyfriend."

Brock looked flushed. "Mom! Don't exaggerate."

"Who's exaggerating?" She looked at me with her worried eyes. "You'd take good care of my boy, wouldn't you, Logan?"

"Mom, please!"

"I'm just saying. Logan looks like the right sort for you. The kind of man who would be able to calm you down, to bring you home more often—"

"Mom!"

She hushed then and tended to Raymond. I felt the eyes of everyone around me and Brock focused on the two of us. Some of them weren't looking directly at us, but they were staring just the same. This was a family whose silence was more oppressive and demanding than their words.

The thought occurred to me—and I don't know why I had never thought on it before—that in all the time I had dated Curtis,

I had never met a member of his family. He had only ever mentioned his parents, with whom he seemed to have had a wonderful relationship, a few times a year. There had been no invitations to holiday gatherings, nor had any of his family ever stopped by for a visit. He had, of course, met Lucille and even my father. I had no reference to measure if this lack of familial interaction was strange, though I suspected it was. Not meeting his parents hadn't fazed me until now, however. Curtis was, to me, almost too manufactured to have had parents. He was put-together and pleasant. He was Curtis of the Boxes. If he broke, I could simply order another.

Brock seemed unable to stomach the silence that had situated itself around us. It was, in truth, more unbearable than any yelling match. "Excuse me," he said as he rose and walked toward the end of the deck. I waited a minute—a few seconds, really—and followed.

He was standing with his hands in his khaki short pockets, staring onto the water accusingly, if not with fear. "My mom and I have a hard time relating," he said when I was there beside him.

"That's not strange. A lot of people have difficulties relating to their parents. You've met Lucille. 'Relative' can be a presumptuous word."

He pointed out to the middle of the lake. "It happened out there. The accident."

"Your father's accident?"

"We were boating. I was never a good swimmer, which, as you can imagine, was astounding to my father—and everyone who knew me, for that matter. You'd expect the son of a champion swimmer to follow in his father's wake. But I never got into it. Not like my brother and sisters.

"So, we were on the boat. My brother, my dad, and me. Everything was fine. I was having a good day, actually. I remember thinking that with some surprise, because it had become a rarity for me to have a good time with my family. Even then I was drifting from them and they were always trying to reel me back. To be more like them. But then Dad started in on me hard about swimming. Why didn't I like it? What was wrong with me? He yelled and I yelled back harder. Mom was on the dock, wondering what was going on.

"Then my brother, who had always taken my dad's side in everything, gave me a shove. I fell overboard and went under almost immediately. Dad dove in after me and pulled me back up, but I was flailing. I was terrified."

Brock was nearly whispering now. I had to lean in to hear what he was saying. I was uncomfortably conscious of the silent group of people further off behind us.

"I was certain I was going to die. It's strange when you've gone under. You can see the light above, its beautiful refractions through the water. But you can't get to it. So much terrifying beauty. And I was so damned scared.

"I was still freaking out when my dad hoisted me up on the boat. I could hear Mom screaming from the dock. Then, as my legs were lifted aboard, I kicked. My dad's head snapped back and hit the side of the boat. He climbed aboard, dazed, and then fell down. He'd had a stroke. I'd given my father a stroke."

I said nothing. Really, what could I have said? That did not compare with anything I had ever gone through. So I stood there with him and stared out at the water as well. Eventually he shook off the layer of regret that was covering him and gave me a bright smile. "Thanks for listening," he said.

Yet it took some time for him to fully come around. This place was his box. And I could tell he had never come out of the water. Not entirely. He was still in that lake. He was still wrestling with it.

The rest of the day was spent walking the cabin grounds and strolling around the lake. There was a small shop on the opposite side that sold colas and snacks. It reminded me of a state park cabin and was more in line with what I thought Brock had meant when he said "family log cabin." Around noon we made our way there and sat at the picnic table outside the shop, under the shade of the trees with a fine view of the lake. Brock was much more subdued at the lake cabin than I had ever known him—which, granted, had not been very long. He was reflective, and this surprised me in that I, ashamedly, had thought the only form of reflection he was interested in was that of himself in a mirror.

"Sorry about my mom this morning," he said, sucking cola from a straw. "For all of her presumptions and insinuations about me and you."

"Don't worry about that. Besides, maybe I would be good for you," I said. I played the statement off as frivolity.

"You probably would. I could use a bit more order in my life. A few more routines." He winked. "Why are you like that anyway? What's the psychosis behind all that neatness?"

"Lucille," I said. "She was and is a mess. Not literally. I mean, kind of literally. She liked to drink. Still does. All my gay friends love her, if that gives you any idea how much she loves the sauce. But when I say she's a mess, I mean that she was always losing things when I was growing up. She'd misplace my schoolbooks, Dad's paychecks, any important letters, her own jewelry and keys. We were constantly in danger of being foreclosed on because she had forgotten to do something or send something in. And it's not like she had any mental issues. Lucille was and is as smart as anyone. She has just always been more careless than *everyone*. I grew up having to keep track of things to make sure we made it to the next week."

"And the lists began."

"I needed order. My parents didn't give it to me, so I instilled it in myself."

"For some reason—and maybe this is because of my own youth—I thought your list-making would be the result of something more tragic."

"No." Then I stopped to think. "Though, whenever I think on why I make lists, there is one memory that comes back to me over and over. It happened when I was around four or five. As I've told you, we lived in a little farmhouse. My parents still live there. There was a lot of space for me to play and be a kid. I was surrounded by a big yard, wheat fields, and a creek that ran down the center of the woods near the house. I didn't have a lot of friends, so it was nice to have all those acres to myself where I could invent playmates and adventures."

"I never had any space to myself," Brock said. "My brother and sisters were always around."

"I was alone mostly." This thought was not a painful one. "As I was playing near the creek one day, it began to rain. Being as young as I was, you couldn't expect me to know there was a storm warning issued. I guess you couldn't expect Lucille to know that either, when she ushered me out the door and told me to go play. It rained real hard for a bit, making a ruckus with the tree canopy, and then it quit suddenly. I came out of the woods and saw that the sky had turned a strange orange color. Everything was tinted and there wasn't a sound to be heard. Not a bird or a breeze. Then I saw it. A twister in the field. It wasn't huge, but I had never seen one up close like that, so it was still pretty terrifying."

"My God!"

"Close to it. At least to me. I was in awe of the big gray monster as it danced toward the house. It roared at me. I ran back to the house, trying to beat it there, as fast as my little legs could carry me. By the time I got there, I had nearly been carried away twice by the strength of the winds. I ran through the house calling for my parents, but was unable to find them anywhere. I was about to head out to the cellar—"

"You go, Dorothy Gail."

"—when I found myself awed once more. Around me—and you'll appreciate this, as it fits my poetic nature—flew papers and pillows and little doo-dads in a kind of frenzied ballet. I don't remember thinking I might die. I don't think those type of thoughts enter the heads of five-year-olds. At least not back then. But I was amazed that I was still standing as the world whirled. As everything came apart around me."

"Did you find your parents?"

"They found me. Lucille came rushing in from the cellar and grabbed me out of my stupor. The house only sustained minor damage, but there was now a ditch in the field next to us. I didn't have a single scratch on me, though."

"Goddamn, Logan," Brock muttered.

"What's wrong?"

"That's what you should be writing about. That kind of awe. That *life*."

And he was right. There was, however, a flaw in this logic, and he knew it as well as I. You see, while life may win you

Pulitzer Prizes and respect from pretentious luminaries, it is rare to ever make you a living. People choose the books they read, for the most part, based on a world they wish for, not books anchored to lives they are familiar with. We nodded this fact in silence.

BY SATURDAY night, the mood at the cabin was more subdued than it had been the night before. The heavy partiers had all gone home and those who were left were content to sit by the lake and talk the sun down as they lounged in comfortable lawn furniture. I stayed up with Brock for a while, but eventually excused myself to head to bed. Before I had made it inside the cabin, though, Brock called for me to wait and we went up together.

Neither of us was really as tired as we should have been, so we lay in bed, curled up close and cuddling, flipping through a thousand television channels in the dark. Brock finally settled on a ghost-hunting program, one of four that was on.

"I hate these shows," he said, peeking out from behind the cover like a frightened child. "But I watch them anyway. It's like flagellation. Still, as long as I have my trusty blanket here, no ghosty can get me."

"They're a total put-on, Brock. They're staged, all of these shows."

"Maybe. But ghosts are real, dammit. Yes sir, they are."

"You've seen some, have you?"

"Don't grin at me like that, disbeliever. Why, I would not be surprised if we're being watched by a ghosty this very moment in this very house." He looked at me with big, creepy eyes. "I've seen them," he whispered. "I've seen them."

Now, I've never believed in ghosts, but neither did I particularly care to hear about them in such a hushed, childlike manner. And when his eyes grew larger, as if he saw something right behind me, he nearly had me. I turned my head slightly. He started to laugh even before he dug his fingers into my sides and shouted, "Gotcha!"

He stood on the bed and began jumping around with the blanket over his head. "I'm a big ghosty! Woooo! I'm gonna getcha!"

I pulled him back down and threw the cover over my own head. Said I, in the most mischievous voice I could muster, "I'll haunt *your* night, Brock Kimble!"

Before he had a chance to respond, I pulled down his boxer shorts and my lips were tight around his dick. I had not intended for the night to take this turn, but how could I control myself? I felt the meat, warm and hard, as it worked its way into my throat. I wanted to wring from it, to suck from it, all that made it thick and—Lord forgive me—juicy. I gave the slit a few quick flicks of the tongue when it escaped my mouth and welcomed it back in greedily. Brock was wrestling with the sheets, tearing at them with one hand as the other guided my head up and down. My tongue traced the glans and I pulled gently on his sac, which made him moan most agreeably. Brock had an average but lovely dick with a very large dick head, and I remember thinking on our first sexual encounter in the park how painful it would be to bottom for him. But now… now I found the idea alluring.

I pulled myself up so that I met his eyes. He knew what I intended to do and he grinned. I kissed his lips and then positioned myself over him. We self-lubricated with precum and spit. The slow, anxious slide onto him was comparable to nothing I had ever done. I was to be divided in two, right down the middle, like a block of wood split by a maul. The sensation was dangerous, and danger was something foreign to me. With every attempted slide down it became easier and less painful, until we were galloping at a distracted speed. The warmth that spread through me was like a ball of energy ready to explode, growing, growing. Tiny particles of heat prickling and riding my nerves. And then at last I came all over his chest.

I stared into his face as we finished. Sweetness. Lust. Candy. Love.

Love.

When he opened his eyes and stared into mine, I knew I had made a mistake. I was in love.

the valley of decision

WE TALKED less now.

I pretended to sleep most of the ride back to Adbury. The music I had brought along proved helpful in alleviating the awkward tension when played very loudly. Neither of us sang along, though. I caught a glimpse of his profile while he was driving and I sighed. I covered it with a snore, as if I were napping.

Even our online conversations were strained and wire-thin, covering the basics of my manuscript and little else. Everything that needed to be said was just under the surface. At the shallow end. One of the things I've found with many writers is their—and I include myself in this—striking inability to vocally interpret their feelings. We find it difficult to say what must be said in the moment it would be most advantageous. Instead, we require pages and space bars, allusions and metaphors. Few writers are the life of the party. Indeed, I wonder if Shakespeare was as socially inept as this.

I loved Brock, and I was aware how that shook everything. My routine would suffer for it.

So, it was at this point that *The Gods Have Jealous Eyes* took another tumultuous turn in story. Maximus threw himself from a cliff in a suicidal fit. Standard, yes. Predictable, absolutely.

But at this point I was certain my book was not destined for greatness anyway. There would be no classroom discussions evaluating my meaning behind line four on page ninety-seven. Off the cliff side, along with poor, lovelorn Maximus, I threw any hopes of rescuing the story. From here on out, I was certain it was beyond hope. Everything I would write would be transparent and soulless. Everything would be scribbling. As I expected, Brock was not a fan of what I had written when next we met, though—oddly enough—he did not express that to me outright.

We were at the coffee shop again. The one with the delicious scones. I had nothing, however, and Brock had only a small coffee, from which he drank sparingly. The shop was crowded with people, but everything seemed strangely muffled. Brock and I were trapped in a sort of stare-off, as if daring each other, or perhaps pleading with each other, to go first and call the book out for what it was. Or what it had become.

"I'm sorry," I finally offered. "It's all I could write." Though the apology must have seemed as layered to him as it was to me.

"I can't do this," he said. He sat straight and stoic, like a man at a board meeting. He even wore a suit. "I can't be involved in a relationship like this. Not now."

"I know. I'm sorry."

"For the book. I know. It's in pieces."

"I'm sorry for everything."

"What's everything?"

"I'm sorry I seduced you."

He paused and nearly smiled. "Your powers of seduction aside, the simple fact is my life just won't allow me to get involved with anyone right now. Not as deeply as you deserve."

"No. I see that."

"And clearly"—he picked up my manuscript and waved it briefly and halfheartedly about—"yours won't either. I'm sorry if I've led you on."

There was a moment where he was waiting for me to assure him that he hadn't, in fact, led me on. But I didn't know the truth. Either way I looked ridiculous.

"You can't change who you are, huh?" I said. It was just something to say.

"I don't know who I am, Logan," he said. His hand was still on the manuscript. "I'm like this book. I'm not finished yet. I'm getting there, but it's a whole lot of work. I've got some major plot holes."

"I knew I shouldn't have tried anything at the cabin, but...."

He smiled. "Well, it was fun, right?"

"Right."

"But fun is all I can do right now. I need to focus on—"

"On what?"

"I don't know. Me. My career."

"That's a lifelong endeavor. It might make it easier if you had someone there beside you."

I felt like I was falling apart, piece by piece. His eyes could see my destruction. There goes an ear. There goes a hand. There goes the heart. I was all over the floor.

"Brock, I agree. I really do. For us to get involved would be a wrong move for me as well." Again, that was just something to say. "But I need to ask you something, and then I'm going to leave."

"What do you need?"

"I need you to find me a new editor when you get back to Hillside. Please."

He sighed. It was a puff, really. And that let me know that his heart, too, had been hit. But instead of breaking, it evaporated.

He nodded and tried his best to smile. I collected my thoughts, my things, and left. The crowd swallowed Brock at the table, so at least I was certain he could not see me as I walked away, shaking.

EVERY writer has a collection—a crypt—of stories, outlines, even full manuscripts, that will never be published. This is a sad truth. While some of these might just be better left locked away, never to be read by another set of human eyes, there's a minute possibility that others might be so brilliant, so ahead of their time that they just wouldn't be appreciated and so are left to fade away in obscurity. None of mine are in this latter category, mind you, but I sometimes want to cry at the great masterpieces the world has never had the chance to see. Think of it. History is filled with writers' crypts. Shakespeare's literary sarcophagi.

My forgotten canon crypt—the tales I kept "just in case" an idea may come in handy at some later date—found a home in my father's old beaten-up army chest in my closet. This is where I went for some kind of comfort after my meeting with Brock. I was still reading through the writings—most of which I had forgotten about—two days later. Nothing was really speaking to me as something I could use, but this was not an expectation I had anyway. I was simply trying to keep my mind busy. I know I looked pathetic—a grown man on the floor in his underwear, surrounded by papers and folders. I know this because I saw it in the full-length mirror I used to get dressed every morning, which was leaning against the wall.

Around noon on that second day, I heard Janey, who had taken the day off work, outside on the street. I rose with a grunt and walked to my window. She stood there, looking quite appealing in a black skirt and white blouse and a pair of classy heels, talking with a pair of young Jehovah's Witnesses, both men. She was playing with a gold necklace, nonchalantly but full of purpose. They were smiling, quite taken by her. I smiled myself. She had them. Soon there would be all sorts of Bible-thumping going on in this old house.

She was keeping an eye out for the Mormons, though. I saw her take rapid-fire glances this way and that. She wanted to keep them interested in her as well. It was entertaining to watch her at times. I never knew how her mind worked, or why she felt such a need to have these two groups of people like her, and I had known her for years. Of course, I knew how it would end. She would simply stop letting them in one day. She would stop answering the door. Feign witchcraft or whoredom. She was in it to get it, and once she got it, she was bored with it. The pursuit was the thing. She would never look at them—these smart, handsome boys—as anything more than a goal. If she did she would have to change who she was.

I WAS summoned to a meeting with my new editor a few days later. At least, that's what it felt like. A summons. A demand. The message was lacking any emotion or pleasantry and signed Frances Barlow. I imagined if it had been sent via regular mail instead of e-mail that signature would have been written in a nearly illegible scrawl that would imply even signing the letter was an imposition. Expecting to see none other than Queen Elizabeth herself behind the desk (the first one, not number two, and looking more Bette Davis than Cate Blanchett), I made certain I was on time. I was early, in fact, and waited a good twenty minutes outside her office. I successfully avoided looking toward Brock's office, though the urge was screaming like a brat child. I watched the clock over the young male secretary until, on the dot, I was called in to see Her Royal Highness.

I was rather startled by how the desk overwhelmed the woman. She was a tiny thing in shades of gray and white. She sat, painfully stern, her face drawn in a natural frown and her eyeglasses set low on her pinch of a nose. Her gray hair was kept back and up so tightly it could have qualified as a facelift. Her gray suit had most likely been set out a month in advance. Truly, the rigidness of the room was something to be admired. There was no play here. This was work. This was routine. I doubted if she had ever lost or misplaced anything in her life. I noticed a neatly lined list on a piece of paper in front of her. Most likely the talking points she wished to hit on with me. This was my element, and I sighed comfortably.

"Have a seat, Mr. Brandish," she said, gesturing with her tiny hand to the chair in front of her desk.

"Call me Logan," I said as I took the seat offered.

"No, thank you. I shall call you Mr. Brandish. And you shall call me Miss Barlow. Not Franny. Not Fran. Not even Frances. And certainly not *Mrs.* Barlow. I was married once, years ago, and it didn't suit me. It's *Miss* Barlow." She did not wait for me to say anything. "The reason I called this meeting was so I could get my footing with you. So I could see who it was I will be speaking to over the phone and where exactly we stand with each another. We needn't meet in person like this all the time."

I sat silent, feeling like a teenager at a job interview.

She gave me an annoyed expression. "Do you understand, Mr. Brandish?"

"Y-yes. Of course."

"Good. Furthermore, unlike your previous editor, Mr. Kimble, I will not be taking you to dinner on the house's dime, nor will I be chatting with you about everything west of the Mississippi or e-mailing you on a daily basis. You're a big boy. You've had enough books published that you should be able to write something without too much help from me. I'm your editor. I'm not your friend or your nanny."

Apparently I looked like a chided schoolboy, because her demeanor softened very briefly.

"Mr. Brandish, I don't say this to be mean. I just think it's important to declare who I am at the outset. I know I can put some people off with how abrupt I am, but I like my rules. Now, I'll be reading up on your other work this week to get acquainted with your style before I dive headlong into your newest manuscript. The one titled"—she looked at her list of notes with a somewhat sour expression—"*The Gods Have Jealous Eyes.* Hmmm. Indeed."

"You've never read any of my work before?"

"No, Mr. Brandish. I'm a busy woman. I don't have time to read for pleasure."

"And you don't want to look over the new stuff I've written?" I held up the folder containing my new manuscript.

"No." Her mouth was perfectly circular. Her eyes were drilling into me. "Not at this time. Let me read over your other work first."

She turned her gaze again to the list before her on the desk. After a long moment, and without so much as a glance toward me, she said, "You may go."

Clumsily, I rose and left, looking back just once as I closed the door behind me. She was already on the phone talking down to someone else.

That night Miss Frances Barlow inspired a rather Dickensian dream. In the dream, Brock appeared at the end of my bed. He was dressed in a long velvet robe and held his hand out as if to encourage me to get up.

"Follow me," he said. He was smiling, and so automatically I rose. "I have something to show you."

Unfortunately, this did not evolve into a sex dream, though it very well could have on numerous other occasions. I followed Brock slowly down the stairs and out of the house into a cool autumn night. He floated just above the ground, like any angel would. The street lamps were lit and glowing mysteriously. Very mysteriously, in fact, because East Second Street hadn't had actual street lamps since the 1970s.

Brock pointed to someone who walked ahead of us, the lone other person on the street.

"Who is it, Brock?" I asked.

"My replacement," he said.

It was Miss Frances Barlow. She walked speedily through the dark, occasionally shooting suspicious glances this way and that, though she never caught sight of the two of us. We followed her a good distance until we found our way to an Adbury side street, known to me because it offered inspiration when I needed a character while writing. There was a pub there called Doyle's that lent itself to scarred hearts and psyches. The door was barely lit from above by a street lantern. Miss Frances Barlow entered and we followed.

As we stood inside by the door, the bar resembled nothing of the Doyle's I knew. Instead, it was as if we had been transported to some seedy Parisian seaside haunt from Jean Genet's literary wanderings. Lit candles decorated every table. They glowed rather than burned in the cigarette-hazy air. There was no other light, so the bar was awash with a dangerous, romantic atmosphere. The music was a lone pianist in the corner, who played with his eyes closed.

The bar hummed with snickering and whispers of rumor. Every now and then a table of patrons—all dressed in very plain attire, suits and dresses—would erupt in a hail of laughter and then become silent almost as quickly. I scanned the tables from where I stood with Brock for Miss Barlow, but she was nowhere to be seen.

"What is this place?" I asked.

"This is the Editor's Den," Brock replied. "This is what every writer has always feared. The dreaded place where editors get together and tell stories about the ridiculous mistakes their writers make. Oh, there are some true horror stories here!"

"It's true?" I was horrified.

"It's all true. Every bit of it."

"I always imagined it a library."

"So did every other writer. That's why it was moved here. But now that you know…."

I turned to look at him, noticing a peculiar menace in his voice. Something deep and dragging. He glared at me, his eyes now glassy and cold. When I looked back at the other patrons in the bar, they too were staring at me with malice and annoyance. Even the pianist had stopped playing.

Then, from out of the back and the dark came the solid voice of Miss Frances Barlow. "I told you I don't want to be your friend!" She came upon me like a rabid mouse. "I don't want to be your friend!"

I began to back up, but the others rose from their tables and began to surround me, as a zombie horde would surround fresh flesh. I looked to Brock for help, but he had joined them. He was one of them after all. He was… an editor.

They began to chant at me as I was cornered. The lone writer, prone to mistakes, cornered in the Editor's Den. "Go write, Logan Brandish!" they sang. "Go write! Go write, Logan Brandish! Go write!"

"I'm trying!" I defended. "I can't! I can't!"

But they continued their chant. "Go write, Logan Brandish! Go write!"

No matter how I screamed, they would not halt their approach. Even Brock. Even Brock. I cowered and saw their hands reaching for me, to tear me apart like pages from a horrid manuscript.

I woke from the dream a wet, panting mess. Feed the Cat, who had wandered into my room during the night as she often does, stood in the door and hissed at me, then ran off. I sat up and rubbed my eyes, looking about for some anchor to soothe my mind. I was angry at the dream, and angry at Brock. Not just Evil Editor Brock in the dream, but Brock in real life. All his talk about me getting out of my comfort zone, and it suddenly dawned on me, though I don't know why it took so long, that he had constructed a perfectly comfortable little zone of his own that he wasn't ready to budge from. He was content to edit, have as much sex as possible, and have absolutely no romantic commitments for the rest of his life. I was furious and I wanted to scream at him. If the sleep aids hadn't already started wearing off, I probably would have. I eyed my cell phone, which was charging on the nightstand beside my bed. In the end, though, I decided against a midnight call.

Still, I needed to talk to someone. Janey was asleep, Brock didn't want to hear from me, and the cat was all hissy. I suddenly wanted to be with Curtis. At least there was stability and comfort there. He would know what to say, and he never minded when I called late at night while I was writing. Of course, it had never been about another man. But no matter. I picked up the phone and dialed. I waited. Curtis never answered. His number had been changed.

persuasion

ONE day I woke up, in as metaphorical a way as it sounds. It was a crisp autumn morning, late September, and I felt like I would lose my senses if I had to wake up one more day to the same ceiling above me. I felt suffocated, pressed upon. Like some medieval torture where I was strapped down and rock after heavy rock was placed on my chest, one atop the other. I had never had asthma, or any problems breathing for that matter, but this morning I couldn't seem to get enough oxygen into my lungs. I tried to breathe in heavy doses, but I just couldn't go deep enough. I couldn't reach down and open up.

At first I did nothing. I simply lay there, accepting it, staring in a desperately pleading manner at the top of my box. I needed to get up. I had my routine, after all. Things to do. So many things to do that were very similar to the things I had done the day before, and the day before that. Yet that which should have offered me some relief or security only made me feel less in control of my breathing. I lay there, the writer in me surfacing, trying to think of some clever way to parallel the shortened days of autumn to the new longing I felt, but everything sounded forced. And besides, I decided that no one said the word "longing" anymore. Who longed? We're all whiners. We have social media to thank for that.

galley proof

In the bathroom, after I had at last pulled myself out of bed, I stood studying my image in the mirror for the longest time. I looked tired and frazzled. My hair was evidence of my restless night's sleep, sprouting from the back of my head like a plant reaching for sunlight. I rubbed at my jaw. I needed a shave. How tedious. Yet I found that I rather liked this scruffy look. It was a thought that had been running in the background for the past week. I decided that maybe once, just this once, I wouldn't shave. The thought made me smile, and so, it was agreed upon.

Furthermore, my hair. Why should I have to neatly comb it just so *every day*? Even on days when I didn't go anywhere? And why had it never occurred to me in all my life to let it grow just a little? Let it have some length. Let it have some... play. Why did I feel the need to cut it so damn short? So neat and perfect. And so, it was agreed upon.

I was practically beaming by this point. Yes. Just a small change, I thought. A small difference to get me through the day. Well, small to other people. It was liberating. I tamed my hair a bit, got dressed in my favorite Kool-Aid T-shirt and my most comfortable pair of jeans, grabbed my jacket, and left for my meeting with Miss Barlow. I felt an amazing thrill, smiling all the way out of Adbury. *Who knows*, I thought. *Why, tomorrow morning I might even paint that damn ceiling.*

As I neared the offices of Hillside, however, a twinge of anxiety began to settle in. What I had written lately was nonsense, and halfhearted nonsense at that. The island on which my book was set had become, in my most recent chapter, inhabited by zombies. Rather, I decided they had always lived there, but somehow had escaped my lead characters' detection, their being so in love with each other. The zombies had eaten the crazy man Caligula—served him up in a stew—and were now after the sweet Flavius and meaty Maximus. These were organized zombies. In my mind, they had lists on the walls of the caves they lived in about what castaway was to be eaten and when.

Miss Barlow's secretary—the wide-eyed and frightened young man fresh out of college who had all but ignored me the last time I was there—gave me a look that said "dead meat" and told me to "go on in. She's expecting you." I didn't even have to wait. As I passed him he said, "Hope you're wearing a cup."

Miss Barlow was standing at the tall window. She was such a small thing, it looked as if the sunlight might crush her. She wore large, ill-fitting shoes that resembled clogs. I wondered how she managed to walk in them. Her arms were folded.

"Sit down, Mr. Brandish," she said. She was smoking. It surrounded her in a vaporous mist.

Finally, she turned to me. "Do you see this?"

"Your cigarette?" I sat with my ankle crossed casually over my knee. I was wearing ankle socks. Before this, I had always worn dress socks to meetings. I hadn't noticed this fact until just then.

"This is a nonsmoking office," said Miss Barlow. "It's a nonsmoking building. There are ordinances passed that make it so a person can't smoke in whole areas of this city. This has been a good thing for me. I've been trying to quit for years. But"—she walked nearer, her clogs whacking the floor like gavels—"your book, Mr. Brandish, your careless attempt at writing, has caused me to pick up the habit once more."

"I'm... sorry?"

"I don't believe I'll ever be able to stop again." She took a long, thoughtful drag and then blew the smoke out in a satisfied and guilty breath, all the while keeping her little eyes fixed on me.

"Of all the writers this house has, and there are some great ones, I get saddled with you. I should sue for attempted murder."

"Oh, come on!"

"And would it have hurt you to shave? Usually when one has an important meeting, he makes himself look presentable. This isn't the mall, you know."

"Am I to be berated the entire time I'm here? Just tell me what I need to do and I'll fix it. Please, let's stall the dramatics."

She let out a breath of laughter and smashed her cigarette into a paper cup filled with water that was sitting on her desk. "Where to begin? First and foremost, get rid of the zombies. You write for men and women of a certain age, mostly women, not college boys and horror fans."

"Fine. But I liked the zombies."

"I didn't." She sat on the edge of her desk, arms crossed like a schoolteacher, jaw firm. "So, I've made you some notes."

She picked up a thick tablet of paper and thrust it at me.

"Notes?" I said, taking it from her hesitantly.

"I read up on your other work, Mr. Brandish. I liked it for the most part. You have given us some good stuff. There were parts of the three previous novels you've published with us that seemed a bit sophomoric, but for the most part—"

"Wait just a goddamn minute!"

"Mr. Brandish, please don't get upset. I'm only trying to help you grow as a writer. To produce the best work you can and give your struggling readership a boost. Read my notes and apply them. They will help you as you sort through the mess you've made."

"I am not in writing class, Miss Barlow. I have a particular style."

"And it is lacking in its current state. You are flailing. Anyone can see it. That writing is lazy!"

"Miss Barlow…."

"Mr. Brandish."

"Miss Barlow!"

"*Mister* Brandish! I'm aware who I am. I'm the best. The best damn editor this house has ever had. You will not have anything but a bestseller under me. Top of the list. Any list! If you don't want to work with me, just say so. But I doubt you'll find another editor who cares as much about our collective image as I do. At least, one that you don't have to sleep with."

The tablet was rolled in my hand as if I were going to swat a housefly. My face was flushed. My feet were now both firmly planted on the floor, ready to leap. But she was right. And, honestly, I felt I was getting quite the reputation with editors of late. No one had actually said anything to me about it, but who would want to work with me if I continued being so difficult?

"I'll look over your notes," I said, rising to my feet. Calm. Calm.

She nodded. "It's in your best interest."

I quickly left her office without another word. I must have looked like a torpedo as I shot past the boy secretary. I stared at the floor, saving my temper tantrum for when I was alone in my car and I could call Miss Barlow any obscenity I wanted.

And it would have been one hell of a tantrum if my thoughts had not been so quickly flipped. I collided—for a collision is an apt description after all, being shot from Miss Barlow's office as I was—with Brock, knocking us both back and nearly off our feet.

I groaned. "Of course I would run into you," I said. "Predictable."

"Like a movie," he said with a smile. He held a folder, which he had managed to keep hold of during the collision. Now, however, he dropped it in play, to go along with the scene.

"Where are the cameras?"

We both twirled around as if looking for hidden cameras and a crew. I covered my discomfort, though not very well, by retrieving his folder for him. He laughed kindly at our embarrassed attempt at humor.

"Are you okay?" he asked. "You look a bit flustered."

"I just had a meeting with Miss Barlow." I burdened the words with heft.

My heart was racing. If my meeting with Miss Barlow was like a punch in the jaw, seeing Brock was a kick in the balls.

"Ah. I see. And Fussy Frances didn't like what she read?"

"I didn't honestly expect her to. But damn! She is a mean woman."

"Or maybe I was just too nice."

A moment passed and we both took breaths.

"So," he said, "what exactly did you write that made her so fussy?"

"I threw in everything but the kitchen sink. And then I threw in that. Why not, you know? There are now zombies on the island and they stewed the crazy guy."

"Well, they have to eat, right?"

"Exactly!"

"Other than your run-in with a snarling editor, you're doing well?" he asked.

"Well enough. How are you?"

He looked at me as if he wanted to say something. As if he wanted to reply with truth rather than pleasantry.

"Well enough," he said, as if the words were broken.

"I better go," I said after another moment. I couldn't take standing there with him any longer. His eyes would unlock me. Unhinge me. They seemed so sad. I wanted to ask about his family and his dad, but he wouldn't allow it. He began to pull away, back to his office.

"You look good," he said before he turned and walked off. "I like the scruff."

In the car, finally alone to deal with the dowsing of emotions I had just experienced, I sat for a time gripping the steering wheel tightly and staring into its center. The silver car emblem there might as well have been a black hole. I wanted to beat the hell out of it, but I was too drained even for that. Finally, all I could manage was a weak growl and then I drove out of the parking garage and on home.

WHILE I was at my meeting with Miss Barlow, Janey had invited into the living room two young Jehovah's Witnesses nearly as adorable as the two Mormons she had previously had in the kitchen. She was conversing with them on matters of faith quite convincingly when I arrived home. Yet, instead of finding this humorous, I was annoyed. I might have even rolled my eyes on entering the room. Feed the Cat mirrored my feeling with a contemptuous stare at the Witnesses as she watched them from the floor and twitched the end of her tail this way, then that. I regretted getting her declawed.

Janey excused herself from the young men and she and the cat followed me into the kitchen. She was giddy. I felt it rush against me in waves as she hurried behind me, ready to burst into giggling at any moment.

"They've been here since lunch," she said. "I should come up with some excuse to make them leave soon. The Mormons are coming by in an hour. We don't want to be in the middle of a gang war, do we?"

When I didn't respond, she continued. "I'm cheating on religions. How crazy is that?"

"That's crazy," I said dryly as I poured cat food into Feed the Cat's dish.

"What's wrong with you? This is funny. This is golden."

I bit my tongue. "You're right," I said. "I just had a bad meeting with my editor today. Really bad. Loathsome."

"You should get yourself a religious zealot. That would cheer you up in no time at all. Want one of mine?"

"Janey! No." My annoyance could not be contained. "Don't you think maybe it's time you stopped with these little games you play with people?"

"Games?"

"Everything you do is in some attempt to gain attention. It's like you're standing up on a chair in the middle of a movie screaming 'Look at me!' Then when you get the attention you so desperately want, you throw people out of your life without a thought."

"What the hell are you saying?"

"Grow up, Janey. Make a change."

"Me?" She was battling, trying to keep her voice down. "Take a look in the mirror, Logan. By the looks of it, that's something you forgot to do this morning. Yeah. That was a cheap shot, but I took it."

She hissed and turned back for the living room. I turned and stared out the window at the yard, my yearning for confrontation momentarily satiated.

To my surprise, just beyond my white picket fence, I saw Grace not so much *in* her yard as she was above it. I stared in complete puzzlement. She was standing on the roof of her back porch, an old addition to an even older house, staring out around her with her hands on her hips and wearing a satisfied grin. Had she flipped? Had she gone senile? I did not have long to question the strangeness of what I was seeing, however, for quite suddenly she lost her balance, her arms struggling to find equilibrium, and she fell right over the edge. I let out a scream of "Shit!" and then bounded out my door as fast as I could.

When I reached her (as heroic as it may seem, I did not believe I had the ability to jump the fence that separates our homes, and so took the long way round, albeit quickly), she was lying on the ground, staring up at the sky, and laughing up a riot. If the fall hadn't killed her, the fit of laughter just might.

"Grace!" I shouted, rushing to her side. "Are you all right?"

"I'm fine," she said between laughs. She wiped the tears from her face. "Just got the wind knocked out of me for a bit, honey. That happens every time I feel a cold breeze up from the river anyway."

She tried to sit up and groaned and laughed some more.

"Maybe you shouldn't move just yet," I said.

She "pish-posh"ed me and slapped my hand away. "I'm not a child."

Janey came tearing into the yard with the two Jehovah's Witnesses in tow. They were carrying their book bags as if something in there might be of any help. "I'm calling an ambulance," Janey said, already on her cell phone.

Grace leaned in closer to me. "Did she bring the God Squad to read me my last rites?"

I grinned. "I don't think Jehovah's Witnesses believe in last rites. That's the Catholics."

"You're right, of course. I forgot. Jehovah's Witnesses. No last rites in that religion. Nor many rights at all, from what I remember." This quip brought on another fit of laughter.

Janey talked on frantically with the ambulance dispatcher. The two young men beside her looked at each other in bewilderment.

"Why were you on your roof, Grace?" I asked, still kneeling beside her. "You have so much to live for." I winked.

"I've never been up there before," she said. "I was out here pulling dead plants from the garden when I rose to stretch. I just happened to see my roof as I was extending my back. The tiles were caught by the sun just so. They shined. And I found myself wondering what the view was like from up there."

"There are windows. You can see the view perfectly well from them."

"That's not the same. Anyone can view things from behind a glass window. No. I wanted to be up *there*. No barrier. No wall or glass encasement. Just me and the wind. I tell ya, Logan, it was exhilarating! You should take a look from your own roof. It reminded me of when I was a girl. I was a climber. I'd climb every tree I could find. Skinned knees and bumps on the head were badges I wore with pride. My youth ain't so much gone as it is folded under all these years and old, old skin."

"Grace," I said, "you're not a young girl anymore. Maybe you are in your head. But your bones aren't going to pay heed to how old you feel mentally. You could have seriously hurt yourself."

"Honey. Listen. I need to tell you something and I don't want you to take it too hard." She put a hand on my shoulder. "You're on the verge of becoming damned boring."

I laughed. "What?"

"It's true. Watch that impulse. It will sneak up on you, and before long you'll be an old man sitting in his chair, all bitter and cussing over lost opportunities."

This made me think of Miss Barlow. Could that be what I was headed for? My stomach spasmed.

"When I used to see you with Curtis," she continued, "I would often hope that you might find someone new. Someone who could get you out of that house more often. Curtis was a nice enough kid, but damn, he could put us both to sleep. Don't deny it. And when you came home with that handsome Brock fellow, I thought—I *knew*—he was just what you needed. He had some spark to him. But where is he now?"

"You really thought Curtis was that boring?"

"He was a pill. A sleeping pill."

Janey rushed back to us. "The ambulance is on its way." She gave a quick glance back at her religious visitors. "I need to see them out before the Mormons arrive. God is keeping me on my toes today, huh?"

"I'll stay with Grace," I said.

Janey smiled and hastened to the Jehovah's Witnesses.

"Mercy, mercy!" Grace chuckled.

"Tell me about it."

MY THOUGHTS were heavy. So heavy I couldn't concentrate on anything for the rest of the day. I had seen to Grace. I rode with her in the ambulance to the hospital and stayed with her until her ankle was looked at and she could come home a few hours later. It wasn't broken and she was fine to walk on it with a cane.

"No more standing on rooftops," the doctor had said.

"Fuck you, Kildare," she had replied.

My plan was to come home and sort out the mess of a manuscript I had before me once and for all. I would come up with a fresh outline, a new perspective. It all sounded good when I was in the hospital waiting room with nothing to do but think. Yet after a while at the laptop, staring at it as if waiting for an answer, I realized the impossibility of getting into any kind of writing groove. I switched off the laptop and fell to my bed like crashing timber. Above me was the dull canvas of ceiling that I awoke to every morning. As was the case that morning, I felt out of breath. This time, however, it wasn't the ceiling that was crushing me. My heavy thoughts were weighing me down now so that I couldn't move from the spot. I looked to my imagination for some respite. I imagined being held by Brock, but that did nothing but snap a chord in my heart.

Finally, I threw a fit. I seized and flung my arms about like a wild man. I screamed and yelled and gritted my teeth and shook my head. I jarred the house. In my head, I was tearing my way out of my situation. I must have looked ridiculous, for when I calmed myself adequately I saw both Janey and Feed the Cat were standing at my door, staring at me.

"Are you okay?" Janey asked.

I huffed, jumped up, and went to the door. "Of course not," I said, and then shut it loudly.

I eyed myself in the full-length mirror as it leaned against the wall in judgment. I liked the scruff, no matter the insults from friends and editors. Brock liked it too. And the idea of growing my hair out intrigued me. And it was this feeling of intrigue alone that gave me cause for concern. For if the mere idea of growing my hair out was what piqued my excitement then maybe Grace was right. Maybe I was a boring man. Maybe I had always been a boring man. Would I, as Grace had proposed, one day join the ranks of the apathetic and miserable?

Then something altogether more horrible crossed my mind. Had Brock found me thoroughly uninteresting? Was the weekend trip a test that I had somehow failed? Did my personal history not dazzle? My life, after all, had been closed off from public view for the most part. I hadn't dated until after college. I had rarely traveled even when given the chance. I always found I had to re-introduce myself at block parties. This was not the life of an exciting man.

Would I want to meet me? Would I want to fuck me?

I mussed my hair and stared into my eyes. I stared hard and long until it was as if someone else were staring back at me. As if my face were a mask and my eyes were those of a stranger. I was taken in by the stare, and I saw desire. It was very clear to me then what I needed to do.

Ten minutes later I knocked on Janey's door, elated and disbelieving. What I had just done was so beyond me, so spontaneous, that it didn't feel like I had done it at all. I was simply watching it happen as some other being took action.

"What's up?" Janey asked. That was my cue to come in. She was in bed but not sleeping yet. A book lay open on her lap.

"Brock said I needed to get out of my comfort zone, remember?" I was pacing and fidgety. I couldn't hide the smile on my face.

"Sure." She looked at me with suspicious curiosity.

"I just booked a ticket to Europe," said I, the world traveler. "I'm heading to Europe and I think I might be there for a while."

Her eyes were wide. "What? Well—how long…?"

"I'm not sure," I said. I stopped my pacing and sat on the end of her bed. "Am I crazy?"

"Maybe. Jesus, Logan. You looked scared as shit."

"I think I am. I am scared as shit and I am crazy."

"So, why are you smiling, you goon?"

I shook my head and shrugged. Then I laughed, and it was a high-pitched, nervous thing. Like a morning bird.

Janey laughed too. She threw a pillow at me. "He said to get out of your comfort zone, dum-dum. Not your area code."

the american

IT WAS not until the anarchist rally that I began to warm to Europe. I had chosen, as my first stop on my European tour, Austria. Innsbruck, more specifically. There was no reason behind that choice other than that's where my finger landed on the map, so that's where I went.

Miss Frances Barlow was, of course, aghast, yelling at me over the phone as I waited in the airport. "I want my book, Mr. Brandish!" I told her I would try to get it to her as soon as I possibly could. "But I'll probably be without Internet capabilities for a bit." And Lucille was grief-stricken that I had not thought to take her along. "How could you not think to invite me? We could make it such a lovely mother/son jaunt!" But the Tennessee Williams aspect that I imagined in that particular mother/son jaunt to Europe in no way appealed to me.

So there I was, at last out of my box. Shaken and dropped in the middle of a strange continent. Thrown to the ground and told to run. My travel experience being so limited, I was not ready for the culture shock. I knew there would be some, but I was betrayed by my ego into thinking I would be able to handle it with class. My life was not a sitcom. But Europe, I found, was so busy, so rushed and filled with things, it did not allow me the time to soak up life in the manner to which I was accustomed: little by little. I longed for my small-town, American existence. Here, everything was thrown at you in a heaping game of catch that no one ever won. I was flattened by it.

Europeans were brisk. They had very little patience for bumbling newbie Americans. I stayed for the first few nights at a B&B in Innsbruck. It was nice, run by a pleasant family, and not too expensive. And not *too* nice. Something along the lines of a Motel 6 with breakfast.

And that was another thing I found it difficult to get used to in Europe. The breakfasts. Yogurt and a roll were supposed to keep me going until noon? I thanked God ashamedly for the Americanization of Europe and the McDonald's He had so kindly planted on every corner. I assured myself that whatever calories I put on at breakfast I would have burnt off by the end of the day anyway. In Europe, one walks everywhere.

And walk I did. Though I had my laptop with the broken U key with me and Wi-Fi all around, I decided it would be wise to stay off the Internet for the first few days so I could devote my full attention to getting to know my surroundings and acclimating to a place that was far from what I knew in Adbury. I had told everyone back home that it might take some time for me to find Internet access and that they shouldn't expect to hear from me right away. A few phone calls to let everyone know my plane had not gone down in the middle of the ocean were all I felt I owed them at the time.

I walked the grand avenues and the charming backstreets of Innsbruck. I walked through expensive china shops and grungy stores filled with bottles of chunky gunk and gunky chunks. All of it, I'm sure, very healthy. I had a nice piece of glassware shipped home to Janey and an extravagant hat sent to Lucille. At night, I even walked the side streets, soaking in the atmosphere, the lunatic children, and the heroin addicts. It took some walking, but after a few nights I was no longer as frightened or overwhelmed. Yet I was also still without inspiration. And wasn't that the whole point of the trip?

Five days into the trip, this in early October, I resumed my use of the Internet on my often-irritating laptop. I sat in my room at the bland, cream-colored desk that I had moved in front of the window. From here I was offered a view of the corner of a building. I looked through my e-mail messages.

Lucille wrote that she was still miffed and "a wee bit hurt" she had not been asked to come with me but wished me well anyway. Janey told me that Feed the Cat had attacked one of the Mormons and this was causing stress in their relationship. I guessed she meant the relationship between her and the Mormons, but it could have very well been in reference to the cat. Miss Barlow demanded some new pages and somehow managed to make me hear her voice ricochet over the miles of ocean and land. Akbar Sobule wanted me to send him five million dollars so he could free his aunt from the Australian sheepherders who had kidnapped her, and as a thank you he promised to send me the secrets to extending the length of my penis. And Brock… Brock said hi.

Agitated by my whole experience in Europe so far, it was probably not a good idea for me to click on to the Amazon page to obsessively check the sales rankings on my three books. But I did, and it was as if the page had poked me in the eye. My heart sank as I saw my most recent book, *Trouble Trouble Trouble*, was no longer at four pretty golden stars but three and a half. A single reviewer had given me one star. Despite my better judgment I read what that troublemaking reviewer had written.

It infuriated me.

From the start, it was clear (at least, clear to *me*) that the reviewer had not read the book properly. As in, open. How could he have? It was clear what I was trying to say. At least, I thought so. But he didn't get it, and this, added to everything else, made me want to thrash back. With every word I read it was as if my stomach was being weighed down with rocks. Big, porous rocks that scratched the lining. I gripped the edges of the desk and repeated the offending words in the review in an exclamatory manner.

"Childish?"

"Mundane?"

"Unskilled?"

And finally the reviewer ended his tirade with "not what I was expecting the book to be about." I sat at the desk deflated, miserable, and wanting revenge. I knew it was unwise, but I wanted to defend my writing. This reviewer had just attacked my baby. My favorite baby. I wanted to refute some of the reviewer's more venomous claims. I wanted to make him see just where he was wrong. Then I wanted to track him down and show him how badly he had hurt me by punching him in the head. Repeatedly.

I decided that—screw it all—I was going to leave a comment on this review for my own piece of mind, and so I clicked on the tag. But to my surprise, someone had beat me to it.

"Try writing a review next time," said the comment. *"Not an attack. Shithead."*

The name attached to it was "Brock." He had no other information on his Amazon profile page. Not a single review of anything, nor any Amazon friends. But I knew this "Brock" was my Brock. He had signed up for an Amazon profile to defend me. I suddenly felt like crying, and not because of the bad review.

THE next day there was to be an anarchist rally in the streets of Innsbruck. It was a lovely day for it. I was at once intrigued to see it and wary of it being so close to me. All that anger and hostility in one place was not healthy. I needn't have worried. The cool autumn air seemed to chill even the angriest of the marchers, these angry activists. People like me lined the streets for the show (and when I say "people" I mean tourists, because the Austrians seemed dead-bored with the marchers). The anarchist rally had been promoted all over Innsbruck by leaflets and electronic media, and I found the forethought, structure, and preparation quite admirable, if a little puzzling—being that, by definition, anarchists were generally opposed to such things.

They were mostly young. Some were dangerously close to being too pretty for this line of work. Many of them looked impossibly thin, as if they had been marching for weeks without rations. This, I assumed, was the style or maybe the point. Their dull clothes sagged off their bodies as they marched in a disheveled parade. There was no interference from the police. They watched with the rest of us. I searched out the faces of the other Americans around me with interest. (You can always spot an American in a crowd of internationals. They shine too much.) I imagined they all felt like me. Awestruck and a bit horrified. I had never been this near to an angry mob and had the distinct feeling that my Americanness would only make them angrier.

There were two faces, however, directly opposite me on the other side of the street, that watched with glee. They were exuberantly cheering on the anarchists. Two women dressed in vibrant attire and watching the proceedings as if it were a gay pride parade. They spotted me soon after I spotted them. The woman with the short blonde hair waved as if she knew me and said something to the other woman, a very tall African American in a very large blue hat. I smiled and nodded at them, and then looked away, slightly embarrassed. When I looked back, both of them were crossing the street, cutting their way toward me through the stream of anarchy as if it were but a busy street in New York.

They came up, one on either side of me, their mouths exposing the brightest teeth in Europe. "Look, Vera!" the blonde woman said. "I told you it was him. Didn't I say it was him?"

"You certainly did," the tall black woman said. She held out her hand for me to kiss. I obliged. "I'm Vera. This is Miss Cassie Bloom."

"I don't believe he knows who we are, Vera. He doesn't know who we are!" Then to me, "We're friends of Cliff's. The gay film star. You wrote that wonderful book for him...."

"Did I Shave My Ass For This?"

"Yes. That was it. Thank you, Vera."

"Mhmmm."

They paused. I was at last able to talk. "You know Cliff?" I asked.

"We're practically *family*."

Vera: "Mothers."

Cassie: "Aunts."

Vera: "Sisters."

"Whatever the relation, you are certainly Logan Brandish, are you not?" It was Cassie who was doing most of the investigating. Vera was keeping her eye on the surroundings.

"I am. I'm here to do a little research. Or rather, get some inspiration to do a little research."

Vera frowned. "Feeling a bit limp in the literary department lately, sweetie?"

"Uh… yeah. My editor… or, well, he used to be my editor…." I saw the quick-as-lightning glances the two exchanged. "He thinks—or thought—that broadening my horizons by traveling would help me out of my rut."

"Mhmmm. Mhmmm." Vera nodded. "He's right, sugar. Nobody wants to read a boring book. You need to keep it edgy and hip. Traveling, seeing the world and meeting new people, that's a surefire way to do it."

"Exactly," Cassie said. "Meet new people and you don't have to invent new characters. Just fictionalize those you have met. Think of all the brainpower you'll save. If you have a religious zealot in your neighborhood, give her a leather fetish."

"A leather fetish?"

Cassie nodded. "The religious ones are the most perverted. It's all that repression. It's entirely believable in a book. Anything is believable these days."

Cassie hooked me under one arm, Vera under the other.

"Let's go find something to eat," Cassie said.

We found a table at a café off the parade route. The noise level was more acceptable and there was no crowd to contend with. My two new friends had drinks in their hands before they even sat down.

"So, are you attached?" Cassie asked once she was situated across from me.

"Cassie!" Vera scolded.

"I have a son," Cassie continued. "And *you* might be just the thing for him."

"I don't think I'm anybody's thing at the moment."

Cassie's face bloomed with motherly concern, and she covered the back of my hand with her own. It was a bit of intimacy that startled me, both in action and in setting.

"I'll be fine," I said. "I'm actually past the whole self-pitying patch. Mostly."

"How do you like Innsbruck?" Cassie asked, reclining once more back into her seat. "How is all of"—grand sweeping gesture—"*this* settling with you?"

"It's not Adbury. It's not where I'm from."

"Wasn't that the point?"

"True. Yes. But I have always been a bit of a loner, you see. I have found that those of us who are loners have a more difficult time *being* alone in new, unfamiliar places."

Vera leaned over the table and looked me in the eye. "You need somebody to sleep with, honey."

"Why, that's it!" Cassie cried in agreement. "Vera, you've hit the idea on the nose. Logan, dearest, you shall come to Rome with us. It's settled. We're heading there tomorrow and you will love it. Rome is the perfect city for writers and artists. It's filled to the brim with lust. You breathe it in like humid air, even in the fall. We could be your tour guides."

"And your pimps," Vera said with a wink.

"What do you say? Doesn't that sound fun? And before you answer, be aware that anything but 'yes' to either of those questions will be viewed as an act of war."

And admittedly, it did sound like fun. And I wouldn't be alone.

After a moment's pause I said, "I've always wanted to go to Italy."

"Everyone wants to go to Italy," said Vera. "It's full of Italians."

"And lust!" Cassie exclaimed loudly. "Oh, Vera! We're going to have such fun with this one!"

THEY had rented a townhouse in Rome for an indefinite period of time. Rome being as ancient and sprawling a city as has ever existed was surely the answer to my artistic blockage. Wherever you stay in Rome, you are always in the center of excess and crumbling beauty. And it seemed Cassie and Vera knew some very wealthy people. We might as well have been staying at the St. Regis, such was the opulence of the place. High ceilings, plush carpets and sofas, and everything gilded at the edges. As with most places of such antique refinement, the rooms were tightly packed with old, moody furniture. Some of the rooms had painted ceilings and it was easy for my writer's mind to imagine the furniture as enchanted patrons who had come to look up in awe and wonder.

Cassie and Vera were the most thoughtful of tour guides on our first day out in the city, doing everything with the flair and dynamics of performance artists in one of the piazzas. They acted out scenes from famous films set in Rome, though I had to tell them eventually that I was unfamiliar with most of the films in their repertoire. I was familiar with the names of Federico Fellini, Roberto Rossellini, and Vittorio de Sica, but I could not recall seeing a single film they had made. The people around us certainly had, though. The two ladies received a fair amount of applause, and they ate it up.

We walked near the Trevi Fountain, sauntering. For one can't help but saunter in Rome, especially if one is American. Vera was haggling with a street vendor over the price of a violet scarf she had fallen "absolutely, desperately in love with." There weren't a great deal of people around us. I was told that the streets of Rome were not as bustling in the autumn season. Cassie said that in the summer, there were times one could hardly move due to the crowds. "And it can get so unbearably hot," she said. "You came during the best season, I think. Good planning."

"It's very nice. Lucille—my mother—she would have enjoyed it. She was so mad I was not bringing her along. Well, mad in her own polite way."

"Sometimes we need a break from everything and everyone we know. Perhaps you can explain that to your mother. Sometimes we have to be the stranger in town and scare ourselves silly."

"That's something I'm finally beginning to understand." We found a table in front of the fountain to sit at. "I can feel my blood pumping through my body again. Back in Adbury, I can't say I would have even thought that feeling was possible anymore."

"You're finally living. I think your mother would understand."

"She might. But she'd forget the next day." I laughed self-consciously. "You remind me of Lucille."

"She likes to drink, does she?" Cassie gave a wicked grin.

"No. Well, I mean, yes. She does. Sometimes excessively. But I think you're exactly who she is on the inside. She just wanted to experience life, but never really had the opportunity. She was given rules to follow and followed them the best she could. She married the man she was supposed to. They're friends, but have never really been husband and wife. Even I could see that as a child."

I was quiet. Things were clicking in my head. Right into place.

"You sound like my son, Jason," Cassie said. "He's still trying to figure *his* mother out too. And he often has that same look on his face."

"What look is that?"

"That if he could just stare a little bit harder at a problem he might find the solution. But solutions to those types of problems are hard to find, because they're so locked up in other people's minds and hearts."

Vera rejoined us at the table, waving her newly acquired violet scarf.

"Did you get a good deal?" Cassie asked.

"Who knows?" Vera replied. "I was doing more flirting than haggling. I think I have a date."

"We need to set you up on one of those," Cassie said to me. "In this city, in this country, you should take a cue from Henry James. Are you familiar with him?"

"Of course," I replied. "Required reading."

"He often visited Italy. And apparently he had a lovely assortment of men to play around with too. His 'Dearly Beloved Friends'. That's what you need. Some 'Dearly Beloveds'. More than one. A whole slew of them just to play around with." Cassie rose. "Let's go find you some men."

"Now?"

"There's no time like the present," said Vera.

She and Cassie flanked me and from there we walked, we sauntered along the ancient streets of Rome, looking for new possibilities. I felt foolish, yet I could not help but like that feeling. My blood was pumping. We didn't find anyone—not that day—but we caught sight of some lovely... architecture.

Nights at the townhouse were such that they made up for every college party I had ever missed, only not a house light was dimmed. The brightness and laughter bounced off the old orange walls and crystal chandeliers and echoed out the open windows into the streets of Rome. We swam in alcohol and spirits on those nights. Cassie and Vera were amazingly acrobatic when soused. Not a single wineglass was shattered nor one drop of liquor spilled. The same cannot be said for me. They donned extravagant costumes—Salome, Lucrezia Borgia, and many others—and invited the most interesting people, some of whom looked very distinguished, and some of whom looked questionable in their motives. Indeed, some of whom looked questionable in their very claims to be human at all, with surgically modified bodies that included horns and whiskers. I imagined this level of variety was what it was like in the great cities of the world in the early twentieth century, when great artists and writers and bohemians gathered, drawn to one another by some scent of sameness.

It was on a night in that first week in the Eternal City that a handsome letter carrier came to the townhouse. He had brought a package for Vera (who, that very day, I had discovered had once been a man, at least physically), but had been encouraged by the ladies to stay a bit longer and play. Cassie, Vera, and their friend Veronica were quite persuasive in the art of temptation. Though I don't know how much persuading was necessary. At first sight, he had surveyed the party with a look of wonder and anticipation. His name, this pretty little letter carrier, was Marco, and he would be my very first "Dearly Beloved Friend."

Marco had dark hair trimmed short and an innocent face, with eyes like emeralds and full, pouty lips. His dark blue uniform looked a little old-fashioned, and I was a bit surprised that letter carriers still existed at all in this world of LOL and OMFG. He wore a double-breasted jacket, tapered at and just above the waist. His slacks were fit beautifully to his thighs and ass, as if professionally done (a true possibility in Rome). But none of that mattered for very long, for an hour later the two of us were in one of the smaller sitting areas away from the party, naked and knocking over porcelain figurines. He was a hungry man, shorter than I, and with the most flexible and curious bright-red tongue I had ever known. A tongue that, I found, could summon magic. Oh, the places it went! Before too long, all the foreplay was over and the grasping and the clutching of agitated fucking began. We shook the walls bare of their ancestral paintings, and I at last was rid of some of the pent-up frustration I had been holding onto since the last time I had seen Brock.

But I held back as well, not wishing to spend every last drop, and for a couple of reasons. One was that I didn't want to seriously injure my new friend. In my fucking frenzy, that was not an impossibility. The other reason was that I needed that longing, that slow-burning torture, for my writing. Or so I thought. For what's a writer without longing?

MY WRITING—the reason, or the *main* reason, for my Grand Tour—had slowed to a hen pecking. My laptop was beginning to collect dust. I was even forgetting to check my e-mail, and my blog…. What blog? This was due, in large part anyway, to the glorious company I kept. Cassie, Vera, Marco, and the rest of the Odd Assortment, as I called them, were liberating in the extreme.

My routine—and I did try to stick with it, at least for a while—was obliterated by the second week of my trip. I had no desire to write an adventure/romance novel when the real thing seemed to have landed in my lap. For once, my real life was better than any fiction I had ever dreamed up. I was having fun. I was eating when and what I wanted. I was having sex. Lots of sex. It was a (nearly) guiltless heathen existence.

The ladies constantly asked how the book was coming along. They called it my *"Eat Gay Love."* Vera thought this was very funny and laughed delicately, followed by "Mhmmm, mhmmm." I answered that it was going well. That I had been inspired by their beauty and their grace. They accepted the compliment, though I doubt they believed it.

Finally, after another furious e-mail from Miss Frances Barlow, in which she accused me of outright laziness and ingratitude to the publishing house, I decided that I needed to get some serious work done on the manuscript if I was to ever get her off my back. The only way this was going to be achieved was if I had a place of my own, barred from interruption. Marco thought this was a good idea. "A new place for fucking," he said in his heavily accented English.

The ladies were saddened by this, however, offering to set thugs and government agents on poor Miss Barlow. But eventually they came to understand and even helped me search for a place of my own to rent.

After employing the Odd Assortment's help, I found a run-down little place that had the needed charm for inspiration. The ladies were, at first, not impressed, both of them pleading with me to take a hotel room closer to the center of Rome and even offering their financial support.

"You'll get the Black Death," Cassie said. "I guarantee it's still hanging around in this place. Look at those moldy walls!"

I thanked them both for their offers but decided to take the place.

The walls of the shack were a filthy brown, faded and sketched by time. Dust hung in the air because there was no furniture for it to cling to. Still, the water and electricity worked well enough, and nothing screamed "Condemned!" Not yet anyway. I had my regrets at odd moments when I missed the comforts of Cassie and Vera's townhouse, but then I reminded myself why I was in Europe to begin with.

The saving grace of the place, and the thing that made my heart jump when I saw it, was the view out the double doors in back. There, tangled and savage, was a wild, exuberant garden with broken stone walkways that I could already see myself drawing from as I wrote. It was small, but it would be mine.

My first expense for the place was a camping chair on which I could sit with my laptop in the open doorway, in view of the garden, and write. I bought this even before I bought anything to sleep on. (Cassie saw to it that I had at least a nice mattress and acceptable bed linens.) Even as a cooler wind came to Rome, I sat with the doors to the garden open, wrapped in a blanket and drinking warm tea as I began trying to churn out pages for dear Miss Barlow. If you were to ask me what I was writing, I would not have been able to answer you. By this point, my plot was beyond me, having grown and mutated and transformed into something unrecognizable. I was writing just to have something to send to my publisher, and it was out of control. Miss Barlow would yell at me when she received it, I was certain. Or maybe not. Maybe I was writing something brilliant. Maybe my ramblings were the cure for all the world's ills. Writing is, after all, stumbling. I had always felt it was rather like bumping one word against another to see if they sounded good together.

It didn't take long before Cassie and Vera had me out of my cozy shack, though, and headed to a trendy club for drinks. The bald bouncer was a giant, with more muscles than I had ever seen on a man outside of comic-book superheroes. Of course, he wore an outfit of solid black, the sleeves tailored to accentuate his arms, which really didn't need any more help in being impressive. He was surrounded by a horde of admirers—young men who all wanted a chance at Everest. He nodded at me as I entered the place, and his ape-like face took on a gentler quality I did not expect.

Vera noticed my interest. "That's a wicked grin you've got there, Logan Brandish. It's brimming with sin, that wicked grin."

The club was a bit too trendy for me, though the ladies were enjoying themselves. The other patrons seemed to look around the club as if in a competition with each other over who could look the most bored. Boredom, it seemed, was chic as hell here. But I was not without my entertainment. The bouncer and I eyed each other in continuous play the rest of the night whenever he ducked in to check on things. He made my stomach growl. All that meat parading around, daring to wear clothes. I decided that I had some more aggression I needed to let loose. I wanted to fuck every striation on his thick, hard-worked body. I wanted to leave marks.

How he got off from working the front door of the club I have no idea. But he did somehow. Sex is as good an excuse as any for getting off work. He motioned me to follow him. Cassie and Vera were enjoying the amorous attentions of others at the moment, so I got away without questions. He led me to a back room that was reserved for parties and special dinners. There were tables draped with white cloths and there were three columns of stacked chairs. Between the two of us there wasn't a word spoken, English or Italian. In fact, I wasn't even certain he spoke English until later, well into the act. (He did, but not very well.) For my part, I had taken a crash course in Italian prior to my trip, but had learned nothing that would keep me afloat in a sinking conversation.

He peeled all of his clothes off, revealing a completely hairless body. His balls hung low beneath his dick. He began posing for me, and, while impressed by his size, I had not followed him to the back room for a bodybuilding expo. As he flexed, I approached him and began kissing his shoulders and caressing his biceps and backside. My fingers sunk into the folds of his life's work. And then, in a movement that took him by surprise, I slapped his ass. I slapped it so hard the sound reverberated through the room. His smile let me know he was up for it.

I bent him over the table, sinking my fingers into him to pry him open. I was not interested in foreplay. I was not feeling romantic that night. I just wanted to fuck. When I entered him I was not polite. I hit it hard and he grunted and hollered as I pushed harder into him. His ass ate me up. Swallowed me whole. By this point, if a lost patron or club employee had entered the room, I would not have cared. Nothing could have stopped the thrashing.

I used his shoulders as support sometimes, squeezing the traps like reigns. Other times I squeezed hard on his ass as I went in harder and harder, leaving great, red marks when I released the flesh. The noises he made were animalistic. Confrontational. And I was winning said confrontation.

When I decided I wanted to see his face, he was flipped. I massaged his great thigh muscles as I pounded out my frustration. He was folded in half as we fucked, his ankles high beside his grimacing face, a face that held a disbelieving but excited expression—that is, when it wasn't giving in totally to the moment. He would curse in Italian and I in English. We were lovers and fighters. Testosterone kings.

I lost complete control once and smacked his chest so hard he squealed. Seeing that he liked it, I did it again. I pulled at his balls as I fucked him. I bit his nipples and held them in my teeth as I pulled on them. Anything I could think of, we did. How either of us survived is a mystery.

Finally, having exhausted my energy and faceless rage, we lay beside each other on the carpeted floor. Our heavy breaths were the closest thing to conversation we had had all night. We were red from hands and sweat.

"Hey," I said. "What's your name?"

"Roberto," he said, breathing much heavier than I due to his extreme bigness.

"It's nice to meet you, Roberto. I'm Logan. Do you want to do this again sometime?"

a room with a view

WHILE not quite as literary or high-minded, my "Dearly Beloved Friends" were every bit as exciting to me as Henry James's must have been to him. Both Marco and Roberto filled a void, and an intentional void at that, I had come to realize. I was not in love with them, but the sex was freeing. After a short time, I forgot about any remaining routines and lists I had. Routines do not operate with voids.

I am quite sure Henry James never sat at his laptop computer, unable to type a single word because he was so enthralled and distracted by the sight of a stream of sunlight bouncing off his muscular friend's back and bottom as said friend slept. And it is possible, if he were in this writing paralysis, Henry James may have had too much class, he might have been too full of decorum, to put the laptop down and wake his friend up by feeding between the two mounds of flesh due to their resemblance to sweet, golden cakes. But I was not Henry James. I was sick to death of decorum. So, once again I pushed aside any pinching thoughts of Brock and went down on Roberto. The fact that neither of my two new playmates wanted anything serious helped matters immensely.

Though I was being well-fed in some brand-new and exciting ways, this did not mean that I let my life's other, older storylines wither away. Janey kept me well-informed by various electronic means about what was happening back in Adbury and, indeed, the world at large, since I had no television. I also refused to buy one of the English-language newspapers, and this was not out of some snobbery, but simply because I preferred ignorance and bliss over concern about worldly affairs.

"Oh, the things I've gone through! Mother fuck! Goddammit!" Janey said one day as I lay naked with Marco on the floor in front of the garden doors. Marco's fingers strolled over my abdomen as if he were playing an instrument. Over the distance, I could hear it was storming in Adbury.

"Losing your religion?" I asked.

"Both of them! They discovered I was cheating on them. I think somebody squealed on me. I'm betting it was that bitch Witness who I've seen walking this street alone like some… streetwalker. I'm so mad I could scream."

I couldn't help but laugh. Marco smiled as my abdominals trembled with the giggling. He began kissing my stomach tenderly.

"What are you going to do?" I asked.

"Well, they came to the house together against me, both the Mormons and the Witnesses, and gave me an ultimatum…."

"An old tomato," I said, remembering one of my many childhood "mis-heards."

"Whatever," she said, pushing away my jest. "They cornered me—literally cornered me in the front room, the goddamn four of them—and said I had to choose between them. Whose god was I going to side with? It was very intense. I didn't know what to do. I was so humiliated and angry, and not even the cat was coming to my aid. She watched it all without a hiss."

I missed that cat.

"So, I just ran."

"You ran? Where?"

"Right up the stairs. I ran, pretending the hysteric, and slammed the door to my room. I stayed in there, wailing like a beaten child, until I heard them leave. Then I could stop pretending like I was crying."

"Pretending? Are you sure?"

"Of course I was pretending," she said with an edge. "I baked cookies afterward."

"It *was* a big project, Janey. Nobody would blame you for becoming attached…."

"Fuck. That," she said. "I don't need them or their gods. I'm fine. I'm just fine right here on my own."

There was a betraying pause. I knew her well enough to know that she was biting her lower lip.

"Anyway," she said. "I better go."

"All right, sweetie. I'll talk to you soon."

"Oh, wait!" she said suddenly, nearly a scream. "I forgot to tell you. Brock has called asking how you are a few times. We've actually become quite chatty. I tell him you're fine. I tell him you're having a blast there without him."

I sat up as if a lead ball had just been dropped in my lap. I hadn't heard from Brock in days. Maybe closer to over a week. Not a single message in my e-mail. "Brock has called?" I sounded panicked. "How many times has he called? What did he say?"

But she had already said good-bye and hung up the phone. And there I was, on the old floor of a rundown shack in the arms of a naked Italian who was now nibbling on my neck. I found myself thinking "Fuck me" in a plurality of meanings.

My new friends and I met in the Piazza Navona that day for something to eat and drink at one of the many cafés. Not all of the Odd Assortment was there, but those I had grown fondest of all made an appearance. Marco and I did not need to wait long for our friends. Cassie and Vera were the first to show, both in dazzling new fashions they had just purchased after seeing a fall fashion show for spring wear.

"We set the trends!" Vera proclaimed.

They had two others in tow: Gio, a shy Italian who had been raised in the States, and Veronica, a British painter with eyes that spoke of apathy or drug use. Roberto arrived last. There was a chill in the air, but it wasn't wholly unpleasant. All but Roberto were dressed in long sleeves and/or jackets. Roberto wore a fetish net top from which his nipples protruded and a pair of shiny, tight leather pants.

We ordered and the food and drink came and went, continuous and slow. Conversation was pleasant, sometimes mocking, but always interesting.

Finally, after Cassie and Vera had finished telling the rest of us about the various inhabitants of the street on which they lived back in America (with exaggeration, I'm certain), the group's attention turned to me.

"Book," Roberto said. Roberto spoke his limited English in single words mostly. He barked them, and this way of communicating reminded me all that much more of a big, sweet gorilla. Marco was there to fill him (or us) in on anything he (or we) didn't understand.

"I think Roberto wants to know how your masterpiece is coming along," Vera said.

"Yes. Do tell." Veronica spoke in sleepy syllables. Every word was connected to the next without pause and with very little concern for punctuation.

"Well…." I didn't know what to say. I was writing, but I couldn't remember a word of it. I seemed to zone out and type of late. "It's getting done, with or without me."

Cassie laughed and picked up her drink. "Indeed," she said.

"I don't know what's happening with it. I really don't. I'm afraid I need an editor badly, but I'll be damned if I admit that to Miss Frances Barlow."

"So, what will you do?" Marco asked.

"I was thinking about that. I have a friend here in Italy. Well, an acquaintance, really. Calling him a friend would be stretching it. Another writer. He moved here a while back to get away from things in the States. The trappings of fame, or something. Bradley Homlick is his name."

"Oh, yes," Cassie said. "He writes those books about Key West."

"I'm unfamiliar," drawled Veronica.

"You know," Cassie said. "*Tales of Key West. More Tales of Key West. Even More Tales of Key West*…."

"Still not ringing a bell," Veronica replied. "Maybe I need a drink."

Cassie continued. "*Even More Tales of Key West Part 2. Even More Tales of Key West Part 2: The Sequel*…."

"How terribly clever," Vera snipped.

"He thinks he is," I said. "And apparently so do a lot of other people. He sells very well. Obnoxiously well, in fact. I occasionally chat with him online. I'm going to meet with him tomorrow. Maybe he'll supply me with some needed inspiration."

Marco was explaining everything that was being said to Roberto as the conversation progressed.

"Sad," Roberto barked.

"Excuse me?"

"He's right," Cassie said. "You do look a bit down. What else is bothering you, sweetness?"

"Am I that obvious? Who needs a book when you read *me* so well?"

"Is this concerning Brock?" asked Marco. "The phone call you got today from Janey?"

Vera leaned forward in her chair. "What's this? News on the romance front?"

"Kind of. She told me Brock had been asking about me and that she told him I was doing great."

"That's good, right?" Gio asked, looking a bit unsure if he was allowed to speak up. "That's what you want. To have your past relationships know how well you are doing."

"I bet he's as jealous as all hell," Veronica moaned with a sneer.

"Maybe. But—"

"But," Cassie cut in, "you don't want him thinking you're doing *too* well without him. You don't want him thinking he could never have you back."

"Exactly."

"Did you fight for him, Logan?" inquired Cassie. "When he said he no longer wanted to pursue a relationship, or whatever it was the two of you had together, did you fight for him? If you fought for him and you lost him anyway, well, then you did what you could. Otherwise you just gave up. So, did you fight for him?"

And there it was. The truth. I hadn't fought for him. I hadn't even tried to move things on to the next level. I had wanted things to progress, but I was waiting for *him* to initiate. When he didn't… I had given up. It was a devastating realization for me, and it showed on my face.

"Sad," Roberto said. "So sad."

BRADLEY HOMLICK was one of the few writers I knew who had become very successful by bucking the norms and writing exactly what he wanted. He must have had one hell of an agent or a very easygoing editor. His books were filled with large casts, crazy goings-on, and a lot of sex, gay, straight, and in between. They were not literature, but then, these days, what's literature? Genre definitions have gotten to the point where you need a dictionary before you head into a library.

When Bradley showed up at writing conventions, he was a star and he was never without a dog—of which he had many—held tight in his arms. He was also always escorted by handsome young men, something that without his fame he might find quite impossible. I had first met him casually via some social media outlet (Facebook, I believe it was), eager to complain about some movie star he had met and how they were not quite as cool as they seemed, before he moved to the Italian beachside village of Viareggio to supposedly get away from all that. Ashamedly, I found his gossip entertaining. He maintained a blog that gave tabloids a run for their money. We had kept in touch through the Internet, which he seemed always to be on.

Viareggio was a charming town, and very relaxing. I could see why Bradley would choose to live there. I took a train from Rome and followed the directions he gave me to his home. I noted the lovely view of the Mediterranean Sea and, expectedly, the boys who played along it in the sand. Bradley's home was an old place, possibly seventeenth century, maybe earlier. He hadn't lived there for very long, so I'm sure to him it still had the smell of other people and their happenings. I was met at the door by a young man with beautiful, sad blue eyes and hair that looked waxed into place. He led me quietly down a long corridor and into a great room meant to impress with its vaulted ceiling and wall-to-wall portraits and paintings. At the center of the room, sprawled on the couch like an emperor in a white robe, was Bradley. He held a small poof of white I discerned to be a Pomeranian, while four or five other dogs sat comfortably near him on the floor. They were all well behaved. I didn't hear a single muffled bark or growl. They had no interest in me.

"Logan!" He acted surprised I was there. "How wonderful to see you! What a lovely thing, to come visit me! Come! Sit!"

Bradley had gained quite a bit of weight since I had last seen him (once at a book convention). His face was sagging and fleshy. He gave a nod to the young man, who subsequently left us.

"Hello, Bradley," I said, taking a seat in an antique armchair. The room was over-scented, like a field of slutty roses. Very slight piano music backed the scene, coming from a hidden device. "Beautiful home you have here."

"It will do for now," he said with a satisfied grin. I had given him something he wanted: appreciation. "I would love more windows, though."

The young man who had met me at the door came back with a tray of drinks. He served them and then departed once again.

"Gorgeous, isn't he?" Bradley said. "But then, they're a dime a dozen here, the pretty men. The only real issue I have with this one is all the downloads."

"Downloads?" I took a drink and grimaced slightly. It tasted more like an aperitif than a beverage.

"The book downloads. That boy doesn't own a single real book. Not a single one! I've seen his room. He just downloads them onto his reading contraption, one after another. It's quite a betrayal seeing that he works for *me*, a best-selling author."

"But at least the work is still being read."

"At a greatly reduced cost!" He was getting excitable. The dogs squirmed. "You can't tell me you prefer electronic media to the feel of real paper. I don't know a writer who does. Not any *real* writers anyway."

I smiled. "How would you have me answer that?"

"With a sentence."

"As long as it's read, I'm okay with it. Things will even out."

"I'm not so certain, Logan. Until I am, I refuse to let any of my books go electronic. That is in my contract. I doubt my handsome little helper has read one word of what I've written. I think this whole e-book craze is immoral. Against the laws of nature." He gave no reason as to why he thought this way. He nuzzled into the Pomeranian in his lap. "Isn't that right, Mister Fluff-n-Huff?"

He kissed the pooch a bit longer and then looked back to me, having seemingly forgotten I was there. "You're looking shaggy these days," he said. His voice was not kind. I had somehow stumbled over to his bad side in the span of a few minutes.

"I'm trying something out. A new look. I'm afraid I've grown boring."

He put the dog to the floor and it ran off. Or at least it moved, and quickly. I could not be certain the little ball of fur had legs.

"Boring? Maybe. Yes. Maybe so. Truth be told, our conversations online are never very thrilling. And I've noticed your sales are slipping. Maybe a new style will help matters. You've still got most of your looks."

"You've noticed that, have you? My sales slipping."

"Well, one hears things." He drank from his wineglass, completely aware of what an ass he was being.

"When one goes looking, yes. One does tend to hear things."

"What you need is a gimmick." He sang the lyrics from an old song. "*Get yourself a gimmick*! That's all my *Key West* books are. Gimmicks. Every one of them."

"What about art? The art of writing."

"Please! Nobody makes art anymore. Certainly not if they want to make a living. Writing is about creating something that can easily be turned into a movie. That means writing things that are easily digestible. The world's gone to hell, Logan. Wake up! You will never be Henry James. None of us will. We are jesters."

I rose, the lone time the dogs showed me any interest. "Maybe I should go. I feel like I've upset you. This was a bad idea."

Bradley clumsily jumped to his feet, letting his robe momentarily fall open and revealing a big belly and aqua-blue, square-cut briefs. "Wait!" he said excitedly, closing his robe again. The dogs' ears piqued as they looked from me to him. "You'd leave me so soon? But I… I mean, what about the writing advice you wanted? I'm like the Great and Powerful Oz. I've got advice! I have lots of it."

"I'm sure you do. Maybe another time." If I had a hat this would be the part where I would have put it atop my head and then gracefully departed. "But can I offer *you* some advice, Bradley?"

"What? Me? Yes. Yes. I suppose." He was clearly put out by my leaving, and stood clutching the robe closed at his neck and abdomen.

"Get off Facebook. Get off Twitter. Get off every site you're on and forget about your blog. Close it all down for a day and get outside. You're pale as a ghost. This is the Mediterranean. There's no excuse for being so damn Caucasian."

I turned to walk away.

"I'm lonely," he whispered as he sat back down on the sofa.

The writer in me said to keep walking. Just edit those damned pitiful final two words out of the manuscript and keep walking. But the bleeding heart in me had it his way and turned around to face Bradley again.

"I've always been so damn lonely and awkward," he continued. "All my life. I wasn't stupid enough to believe that fame would change that, but… it's a trap of my own making. I want the attention, you see, but I'm scared to death when it's there. When it's staring me in the face. Social media is a safe compromise."

"I understand. I really do. I'm as awkward as the next writer. I'm right up there with Emily Dickinson." Dramatic pause. "But the only way to change is to change. The only way to stop is to stop. And if it helps at all, I've always been so jealous of your success."

Bradley smiled, genuinely for the first time since I had arrived, even if it was a sad little thing. "We're all jealous of someone, darling," he said. "We applaud at our friends' awards, at their triumphs and accolades, but inwardly we are stung."

I left then, having nothing else to say. I put my imaginary hat on my head and left Bradley on his sofa, surrounded by his own self-doubt and loneliness. That stuff is catching and I wanted no more of it than I already had. It amazed me, the difference between how we see ourselves and how others see us. We are all, individually, so many different people—the one our friends see, which our families see, which strangers see, which we see— looking in the same mirror but getting refractions instead of reflections. Perfection is a matter of perception.

Having some time on my hands, I walked along the beach of Viareggio for a bit after my visit with Bradley, shoes in hand. The cold wind brushed through my hair wildly and I enjoyed the frenzy and the chill of it. I heard a laugh carried on that wind to me from across the beach, where a handful of grown men were playing in the sand, apparently calling dares in the cool weather. The beach was barren but for them. One of them wore only a tan sweater and a thong swimsuit. A pair of dark trousers lay thrown on the ground beside him. He was laughing the loudest of them all, and it was that laugh that stopped me where I was. Though muffled by the wind, it was familiar, resembling another laugh I had heard in the not-too-distant past.

I squinted at the group of men as they played—frolicked, that's the word—in the sand. And then I gasped with realization. *Curtis?*

That was certainly his laugh, only freer than I had ever heard it, reaching out across distances and teasing for play. The foppish brown hair was the same. And, yes, that was definitely Curtis's lovely round ass bouncing along in the black thong. He never was able to tan, which was one of the reasons he never went swimming. Yet here he was, his alabaster ass jumping up and down by the Mediterranean Sea.

What were the chances of this? I wondered.

And yet it couldn't be Curtis. The Curtis Little I knew would never be so daring or spontaneous as this. He would never let another man smack his blatantly lily-white ass in public, bare or not. But this man's three friends had all just done so in quick succession. If he had just turned around, I would have been able to tell for certain if it was indeed Curtis. But they were getting farther away, not closer, and none of them noticed me standing there, staring at them. They were chasing one another like children down the length of the beach now, to the far end.

I decided I had been seeing things, possibly brought on by the strange, bitter drink Bradley had served me, and headed for the train station. Still, the laughter stuck in my head and it made me smile. The thought of Curtis made me smile. Not out of any deep feelings of love, mind you, but affection and gratitude.

When I arrived in Rome that night, Marco and Roberto were waiting for me at my place. I found them strolling around outside like conspirators to a kidnapping.

"Bar," Roberto grunted. He flexed his tits, making them bounce alternately. "I dance for you."

"Cassie and Vera said you have to come," Marco said in a voice of finality. "You don't want to upset them. Go get dressed. We will wait… and we will also go through your things to pass time, because we hate waiting."

So, clearly, I had no choice. I was more or less carried into my little home by the larger of the two. While Roberto picked out something suitably slutty for me to wear to wherever we were headed, Marco fixed himself a screwdriver and searched through my small but growing collection of new books and CDs.

I had just enough time to get on my laptop and delete my Facebook account before Roberto shouted "you wear this," having apparently found something that met his criteria for evening wear.

Together, the five of us—myself, the Italians, and the ladies—found our way to a club we had visited only once before and that was ever-teeming with the virility of Roman life. Red-curtained and not too dangerously lit, the club offered a safe eroticism. It was fairly busy, though there had been a noticeable decline from our last visit, when the weather had been much warmer. The volume of the night was high and the air tasted sticky sweet.

Cassie and Vera almost immediately split from me, Marco, and Roberto for the most crowded area of the club. "Ak-*shon!*" Vera sang as the two danced off. It would not be hard to find them at the end of the night. They glittered brighter than the glitterati.

The remaining three of us left looked for a place that was less popular and more conducive to being comfortable, and found it in a back room where four or five other people laughed and drank, scattered around a large center table. The music was pumping through the place, though, and seemed even louder in that area, so we still needed to scream at one another to be heard. Luckily this was not a night for deep conversation, but for dancing and laughing.

Roberto, baring as much tit and ass as he could get away with in an outfit that was little more than net and leather, climbed up on the table and motioned for Marco and me to join him. Marco did not hesitate. I did, thinking a table collapse was imminent, but was eventually pulled up anyway. The two started dancing around me suggestively in prelude to an orgy. We were on stage and a few other club patrons had wandered into the room. I had not the drinks in me to let loose like this.

"Dance!" Roberto shouted.

I moved just a little, like a bobble head, grinning with embarrassment. I blushed neon-bright pink. Roberto mimicked my movement and said again, "No this!" Then, again, "Dance!"

Marco, too, was encouraging me. I looked around for some way out but saw that no one was even looking in our direction, busy with their conversations and shouting matches. I was not, it seemed, the center of the universe after all. I thought of Brock. Of how he had let go and danced like a madman at his family get-together even through his pain. And so, I took hold of the sync beat.

"Here goes absolutely nothing."

And I danced. I danced like I was a crazy person. I remembered Brock's movements, his arms flinging, his head bobbing madly, and I danced an ode to him. I sent it across the world straight to him. It was cathartic. Roberto and Marco howled with laughter and they, too, began dancing in anarchic rhythm. It was the most fun I had ever had at a dance club. Hell, it was the only time I had ever let myself feel the music like that. Just let it take over in a form of possession.

That is, until I poked a scary Italian girl in the eye. I didn't realize I had done it until she began yelling at me over the music and calling her boyfriend—a large black man who was on more steroids than Roberto—over to kick my possessed ass. As the scary woman yelled at me, eyes painted-up Jezebel Hell, the scary, huge man eyed me down, making angry faces and clenching his fists. I apologized profusely as I knelt on the table, giving my best innocent American performance ever. It was then I realized I might not have even hit the bitch in the eye in the first place, for she was won over by my sincerity and began to point at Roberto as the true culprit. An impossibility, because he had been on the opposite side of the table. Roberto, though a bouncer, was a lover. Not, as they say, a fighter. He had no wishes to fight anyone, even if the sight of two beefy men wrestling around together would have been quite entertaining for the rest of us. So, the three of us leapt from the table and quickly left the room without further incident. Once we were outside the club, we burst into laughter.

"What in heaven's name?" Vera said as she and Cassie made their way onto the street with us. The nighttime crowd was thinning out. "We saw you three take off out of there like little gay bats out of a big straight hell. What did you do?"

"My dancing," I said. "It's going to get someone killed."

the awakening

LEAVE it to Janey to reestablish the nightmarish link between religion, sinning, and burning.

Roberto had stayed over at my place. It was morning, and he was completely naked and lying on his stomach across my knees. I was sitting up on the bed, branding his magnificent ass red with eager slaps. *Whack! Whack! Whack!* As I felt his dick harden against my lap with each playful blow, I slapped harder, enjoying the sharp sound of the flesh-to-flesh contact and the delicate after-jiggling of his ass cheeks. Roberto had been a bit of a psychiatrist for me on my trip. He let me tap into my aggression and frustration and take it out on him. Indeed, he had encouraged it. And there had been a great deal of frustration to unleash. A lifetime's worth. But it was beginning to wane. To lessen. It felt as if I were shedding heavy garments every time we fumbled around and every time we bit, slapped, or punched each other. Thank God he never retaliated too fiercely. My face would have caved in with a single strike from his massive paws.

It was in the midst of this playful punishment—just as I laid a particularly satisfying smack across Roberto's hindquarters—that Janey called. Thinking it was Cassie and Vera, with whom I had plans to visit St. Peter's Basilica that day, I answered. It was pointless to avoid a call from them. They would simply call and call and call until you answered. Until you realized that your house on fire was not nearly as important as the paint they had just purchased or a trip into town. Instead of the duo of distraction, however, Janey answered in a worried, mouselike tone. The kind of voice she used with her parents because it always got her out of trouble. The kind that said *Listen to how cute I am and feel pity, not anger.*

I leaned forward as if I were sitting at a school desk, elbowing Roberto's ass. "What's the matter, Janey?"

"The good news is my sex drought is over. I had a threesome." She paused. "With a Mormon and a Witness."

"Are you serious?" I smacked Roberto's ass for emphasis… or, more truthfully, to get one more good smack in. "How was it?"

"What was that noise?" she asked.

"Ass," I answered. "How was it?" I asked again.

"Sex, all in all, is better than I remembered it. I mean, it's been a while for me, and there *were* three of us. That was new. So, it was a bit awkward at first. Then it got really good. Then it got awkward again. And then… um, when the house caught fire, it was just plain scary."

"The house caught on fire?" I tried to stand but Roberto had me pinned. As I was talking to Janey, he was leafing through a magazine I had by the bed.

"Yeah. That's the bad news." She was biting her lip again. "But don't worry. It was just a small fire. The couch is completely gone, though. Poof! And a bit of curtain. And a patch of wall. It shouldn't cost too much to get it repaired. I don't think it will anyway. And we were looking into getting the living room reworked by one of those makeover shows anyway."

"Were we?"

"Weren't we?"

"How did it happen?" My fingers were digging into Roberto's ass. At the moment he was a giant stress ball. He didn't seem to mind.

"Well, you see, me and the boys were playing around in the living room. I decided my bedroom was too intimate a place for what we were doing. We had lit some candles to give the living room a nice atmosphere. It smelled real nice. I thought it would ease them into it. It seemed to be working too. Then Feed the Cat decided to look in on things and knocked over one of the damn candles. She went sprinting for the kitchen, leaving us to die in flames. The goddamn flames of lilac-scented hell."

"So, you got it under control?"

"We did. The fire department arrived just as we finished getting dressed out back. Both Christians were blaming themselves for it, saying this was God's punishment for their sinning. I went along with it, and said they were probably right. It was their faults. That they had led me astray and probably weren't very good Christians in the first place. I wish you had been here. It would have been much funnier."

I began to realize something then. The idea of heading home filled me with such displeasure I nearly gagged. How long could I stay away from Adbury? Could I make a career of it?

"On the bright side," Janey continued. "I have a date with a cute fireman next weekend." When I didn't respond, she said, "Logan? Are you mad?"

"No, Janey," I said. "I'm really not."

"I'm so relieved."

"But damn, Janey! What else do you do in that house that I don't know about?"

CASSIE, Vera, and I stood in the middle of St. Peter's Basilica. We marveled at first. That's what you are supposed to do. How could you not? It hardly seems real, there is so much to it. The architecture, the art, the gold. My God! The shining splendidness of it all assaults the eye in chunks. The basilica was a place designed to make one feel small. Like a mouse in God's bedroom. Each column in the place seems to look down in amused condescension. And that feeling of being judged was why, I think, our moods began to shift from awe to disgust.

"It's so much," I said, still looking up at everything that was looking down on me.

"Every time I come here it's the same," Cassie spoke. "At first I am enamored by the audacity of this place. Its muchness I find attractive. I could wear it as a necklace or a crown. But then, when I think about what the basilica is supposed to stand for— this place above all other Christian buildings on earth—I am filled with the tiniest bit of anger. It seems to me too showy to be sincere."

We walked slowly, somberly, through the crowd. Tourists and zealots.
"How do you mean?" I asked.

"Well, it's supposed to be a place for God, right? God with a capital G. Compassion. Love. Acceptance. All that good stuff. But I've been reading up, and the history of the place is far from Godlike. Vera didn't even want to come today."

This had been apparent. Vera had been giving the building a sneer since we entered. A stink eye for every loudly designed corner.

"It's hypocrisy. That's what it is," Vera said, refusing to keep her voice down. "You want to be a true Christian? Melt down this gold and use the money from it to feed folk. This ain't nothing but a show of domination. I feel absolutely filthy being here." She caught the eye of another American tourist, who did not hold back in giving her a shocked shake of the head. "That's right! I said filthy!" she said to him.

"Take heart, Vera." I tried to calm her. "There are gay men's hands all over this structure. Michelangelo decorated the hell out of this place."

Vera shrugged. And, honestly, I saw her point. This was a hollow show with no heart, especially if you were never particularly religious. Maybe we just didn't "get it." We walked on. What could be done about the past? Lives lived could not be unlived. Choices made could not be undone. And justice? It's a pretty word, but sometimes little more than that.

I heard my name called in a manner that respected the surroundings yet got my attention. I thought maybe it was Roberto or Marco, but when I heard it again (and the subsequent hushes that followed by the annoyed religiosos), louder, I realized that shy call was coming from none other than Curtis Little. I twisted around so fast I could have drilled right through the floor and into the catacombs below.

There he was. Not so much tanned as looking extremely refreshed and fit. He wore a soft white shirt and purple pants (*purple!*) with sandals (something I had heard was against the rules in the basilica), and carried a techno-geek backpack. His hair was in the same style he had always worn it, but it looked blonder, and he had new glasses with thick black frames. He was smiling with such giddy anticipation I was struck momentarily dumb.

"Logan," he said, coming near and giving me a hug. "It's Curtis."

The ladies were intrigued.

I laughed. "I know it's you, silly. I'm just... you look amazing!"

"Oh, come on! I look the same. I've always looked the same. I've seen photographs of me. I'm like Dorian Gray's boring brother. I'm Borian Gray."

The attempt at a joke was something completely new.

"But different. You look different as well." It was astonishing, the change, though he didn't seem to see it in himself.

"So, this is the infamous ex," Vera said with wide eyes and a smile. She leaned back to take a look at Curtis's ass.

"Is it him?" Cassie asked.

"Yes, it is. And perfectly described by our friend the writer," Vera answered.

"Curtis, these are my friends, Cassie Bloom and the Lady Vera."

Curtis bowed and took each of their hands in the manner of a man a century long past. "My ladies," he said with a grin and a playful bobble of the head. "Lady Vera?" he said when he took her hand. "Nobility?"

"Why, yes. I am something of a queen."

"What are you doing here?" I asked. "In Italy, I mean?"

"I'm the company's number-one man in foreign distribution now. Can you believe it? I get sent all over the world. Honestly, I've been having a bit too much fun with the position lately."

"Nonsense," said the ladies, predictably in unison.

"What about you?" he asked. "I never thought you'd leave Adbury."

"That stings," I snapped. "But it's true, I suppose. I was a bit stationary, huh?"

"We both were."

"But I don't think I necessarily ever *loved* Adbury."

Cassie and Vera, realizing they were akin to glittery flies on a very ornate wall, took the moment to graciously bow out of the reunion going on in front of them.

"Well, Miss Vera," Cassie said. "Perhaps we should let these two catch up. We do have a chapel to gawk at, after all."

"Indeed," Vera replied. "Nothing screams 'God' like enormously muscled men wearing tiny fig leaves."

They said their good-byes and headed for the Sistine Chapel.

"They look fun," Curtis said. "Old friends?"

"Brand-new, in fact. I just met them a few weeks ago, though they seem to have known about me for a while."

"Well, you're famous." He winked. That was new too. "So, are you going to answer me? What are you doing out of Adbury?"

"My writing has been less than stellar of late. I came to Europe to find some inspiration, to really dive into the whole creation process. Somehow, though, it hasn't quite worked out."

"Of course not. It's Europe. There's way too much to see. Who wants to be staring at a computer screen all day?" He held out an arm for me to grab on to. "Shall we walk?"

We meandered (such a lovely word, *meander*) out of the basilica and into the spill of the crowd on St. Peter's Square. The obelisk stood alone in the center, a dignified captive from some other civilization. It stabbed at the very heaven that kept it pinned down.

"I thought I saw you in Viareggio the other day," I said. People looked at us, two men arm-in-arm, but I was enjoying Curtis's new brash spirit. "I was there visiting someone and took a walk along the beach, and I swore I heard your laugh."

He blushed a furious scarlet and laughed, embarrassed. "That was me. You didn't see me in my... swimsuit, did you?"

"In your *thong*? I certainly did. The view was, as always, splendid."

"I was with a client and his friends. They were a very flirtatious group. The things I do for my career! Why didn't you come say hi?"

"I had to get back here. Back to Rome. But I stayed and watched for a while, if that makes up for it."

Curtis shook his head and laughed some more. He would most likely remain a shade of rose for the rest of the day.

"Are you seeing anyone?" I asked. I sincerely wanted him to be happy. But—and I admit this fully—I also didn't want him to be *too* happy. Box expo model: Yes. Calvin Klein model: No. We all like to think former lovers never get over us.

"I've dated on and off. Nothing too intense." He paused, and I could tell something important was coming. His words were standing on tiptoe. "Honestly, Logan, splitting up... it was the best thing for me. The best thing I could have done. I hope you understand."

"Well, don't try to soften the blow or anything."

"What I mean is, I was with you because it was comfortable...."

"Safe."

"Right. I didn't have to do any work."

"Neither of us did."

"Right." Pause. "We were so damn boring."

We broke into cackles that scared the pigeons. We continued walking around the square, no longer arm-in-arm but stride-to-stride. The air was cool, but not cold.

"What about you?" he asked. "Do you have a new stud in your bed, twisting the sheets?"

"I was… seeing someone after you and I split." I corrected myself. "Not really *seeing*. That's a strange phrase for what he and I had. I guess I was just testing the waters. I swear, though, it felt like something more than that." I tried to hide the regret in my voice. "Then I came here, and now I'm messing around with two Italian countrymen, Marco and Roberto."

"Alternately?"

"Sometimes." I grinned. "Sometimes at once."

"And how's your writing coming along since you've been here?"

"It's not really. As I said, it's not been going well for a while. There are words on the page. I see them being typed. But I feel as vacant as hell when I'm writing them. My mind wanders. I've got to get it done, though. I keep telling myself that. Work, work, work."

"So, there's no real romance in any form for you here. Not really."

"What do you mean?"

"There's no man. You're playing around with a couple of guys, but that's not romance. And the inspiration you thought you would find here has not surfaced, so there's no real writing either. Logan, what are you doing, then? I mean, what are you *really* doing?"

We stopped walking. I stared at him as if he had just asked me to explain quantum mechanics. "I guess I need to refocus, huh?"

He shrugged. "Maybe. You can still have fun, but don't lose sight of what you came here for. And"—he smiled and pushed his glasses up on the bridge of his nose—"maybe you should cut back on the sex. Sounds like you're becoming a bit of a whore."

I snickered. "Or maybe you're just a prude."

We walked a bit more, chatting about the things we knew together. Janey, Lucille, Grace. He stayed with me while I waited for Cassie and Vera to finish their tour of the Sistine Chapel (which didn't take long, as they were soon kicked out for being too loud), and we exchanged numbers and parted ways again, this time with a hug and a friendly kiss on the cheek.

"Get something figured out, did you?" Cassie asked. "You look like a man with a light bulb over his head."

"Not just yet," I replied. "But I think I'm on my way." I smiled. "Ready to go, ladies?"

"Yes, please!" said Vera. "I think those papal guards over there are undressing me with their eyes. I feel harassed! I might have to ask God to smite them tonight."

WHAT was I doing? What *was* I doing?

Curtis's loaded question—and he had to know just how loaded it was—wouldn't let me be. Was I simply trading one safe existence for another? My life in Rome seemed exciting at the time, but once the novelty wore off and I fell into other routines, other patterns of being, would it more resemble my life in Adbury than I wanted to believe? Was life simply a series of boring moments tied together by fleeting knots of excitement? The thought bothered me. It bit at me. But even more so, I was bothered by the knowledge that I had been fine with a monotonous existence back in Adbury, and that was but a few weeks past. I had not sought out any adventure at all then. I was fine in my safe, contained life. My life as an inhabitant of a box.

The day after I saw Curtis in Vatican City, I took a shopping stroll in Rome. I needed some groceries. I was thinking I might host a small get-together at my little retreat before it got too cold. I could finally put the garden to use, as long as I told everyone to dress warmly. We could roast marshmallows (or whatever it is Italians roast) over the fire pit.

I passed an old bookstore I had frequented since living in Rome. They mostly carried used books with tattered covers. I loved the dim look of the place, trading light for enlightenment. Like all small bookstores, it had a comfortable edge of thoughtfulness and sleep. I had nothing in mind to purchase. I thumbed through some older books, titles and authors unrecognized. I went to the New Arrivals rack at the front of the store, names known to me. And then, as my eyes drifted lazily past the half-off tables, I saw a copy of my little darling, *Trouble Trouble Trouble*, peeking out from behind an Italian encyclopedia of herbs. I picked it up, wiped a line of dust away, and examined it. It looked well-read. Beat up. That was good. There were even a few passages underlined by pen and pencil where someone, or someones, had been touched by the words I had written. There was a victory and a defeat in this moment. I wanted to cry, though I couldn't tell if it was grief or relief.

I bought the book and went on home with it and my other morning purchases from my shopping excursion. I had formed a list in my head, a fragment of the former Logan, of the things I needed to now do in… preparation. Things that had come to me on my journey back from shopping that seemed altogether—and appropriately, so near the Papacy—like an epiphany. I unpacked my groceries and put the ragged, well-read copy of my book on the floor by my bed on the very top of the large pile of other books I had stacked there. I then went to my laptop and saved all the files, all the writing and work on my new work, *The Gods Have Jealous Eyes*, onto a flash drive. I saved the work, but had no real intention of ever looking at it again. *But then, who knows*, I thought. My ramblings therein might, in the future, spark some sort of inspiration. Some surprise *A-ha!* I slid the flash drive into my jacket pocket, and, before turning the laptop off, I looked at the troublesome machine for a long moment. I massaged the aching spot where once reigned the letter U.

"Time to go," I said, and shut the case.

I then called Janey and caught her just as she was headed out the door herself for a parent-teacher conference at school. "I've decided to stay here a little longer," I told her.

"How much longer?" She sounded genuinely disappointed, though the time apart had been good for both of us.

"Indefinitely. I don't know." I looked out at the garden as we spoke. I was planning a party. I was finally going to use the garden, to be *in* the garden. No more just looking. "You should rent out my room," I said. "Make us some extra cash."

She laughed. "Who would I rent it to?"

"One of those Jehovah's Witnesses or Mormons you constantly lead astray, Jezebel."

"Yeah. I imagine their flockmates are none too pleased with them right now." I heard her get into the car and start the engine. "So, are you staying in Italy for a man? No man is worth it."

"Absolutely not. I'm keeping myself open for Brock, that fine fella back in the States. Someday soon-ish I'm going to come back to Adbury and I'm going to fight for him, just like I should have done when I was there."

"Very romantic," she said.

"Like you and your fireman, huh?"

"Fingers crossed."

A thought occurred to me. Though I didn't want to return to the States just yet, I did miss my friend. "Janey," I said, "why don't you fly over here? Soon. I'm having a party. I'd like to see you there. My dime."

"What?"

"I miss you, gal."

She paused. Janey was tearing up. "Shut up." *Sniff.* "We'll talk about it later. You're going to make me run off the road… or into a Mormon."

"Think about it," I said before hanging up.

I called my publishing house next. Hillside. More to the point, I called Miss Frances Barlow, the Queen herself, but she was in a meeting.

"Would you like to leave a message, Mr. Brandish?" her polite young secretary asked. "She's been waiting to hear from you for quite a while."

"I know. And I'm so sorry about that. But tell Miss Barlow she doesn't have to worry about anything anymore."

"Oh, good." From the sound of him, from his great exhale, I gathered that Miss Barlow had been venting her frustrations on the help.

"Tell her that the book is a no-go," I said. "I have decided it's not worth my time to write nor is it worth her time to read."

"Mr. Brandish?" If a voice could have color, his was drained of it.

"If she needs to get hold of me, I'll be here. Maybe we can talk about something in the future, but as for this particular work, I'm done."

"Mr. Brandish! Please. She's smoking. Belching fumes like a power plant. I have asthma, Mr. Brandish. Think of me!"

"Sorry. Have a good day."

I grabbed my laptop, that source of sole companionship and utter irritation for years, and wandered the streets of Rome until the sky grew dark. It was a giddy funerary march with the deceased—or condemned—swinging at my side. I stood beside the Tiber for some time, refusing to allow myself to think second thoughts or question my motives. I had made a decision and I was sick to death of all the goddamn doubting. I just stood there and watched the world draw its shades.

With all the athleticism I could muster, I swung like a discus thrower and pitched the laptop into the river. A pinch of remorse surfaced, but I beat it back down into my core and was then able to enjoy the splash in the distance. I imagined the laptop dissolving into a million pieces, every regret obliterated or eaten by big Roman fish.

The relief, as lovely as it was, did not have time to linger for long, however, for two Italian police officers a few yards away caught sight of my littering and began yelling at me, pointing and gesturing for me to stay where I was as they approached. I did, of course, the only thing a responsible American could do. I ran. I hauled ass. And I was a crafty, dodgy little American too. They chased me for a small increment of time, cursing Roman obscenities I had come to know, and I, as I ran, was cursing American obscenities I had grown up with. I could not help but smile, though. It was my laughter that would have been my undoing if the police officers had pursued me with any real vigor. At last, I ducked into a side street and lost them. I watched, hand over mouth to keep quiet, as they passed by, shrugging once and then turning back for the river.

I was a fugitive. A criminal. I was a freaking bad boy and laws and rules and lists and routines did not apply to me anymore. Brock would have been proud.

a separate peace

EVERYONE has seen those movies. The ones where love succeeds. Where it triumphs over every ridiculous hurdle and hill. Where the heartache, tears, and anger, the acidic regret, is wiped clean with a kiss and a swoop of the dolly. Where the orchestra plays the hell out of a full-bodied string and trumpet score, and the audience is manipulated into thinking, if ever so briefly, that, yes, things like that *can* happen. Everything *can* be resolved just as neatly as that. What we as the film audience are not encouraged to do is ponder what happens after The End. The cynic's cliché: What happens after "Happily ever after." Of course, without asking, we all know anyway.

After the story ends, after the film credits roll—after you close the book on those last words—there will be explaining, and there will be lots of it.

Who'd you fuck and why? Was it to get over me? Did you need to fuck all those guys to forget about me? What took you so long to come around? And if you don't know the answers to these questions, was your storyline worth the trouble at all?

Be here now. Be here now, darlings.

The airport was humming with activity. Activity with an accent, at least to my ears. I was there waiting on Janey. It had been a little over a week since our conversation in which I convinced her to come to my get-together in Italy. It seemed a far-fetched idea at the start, but then she began to warm to it. She needed to get away from Adbury, and we both knew it. Things with the fireman were going well, but at a snail's pace, and the Historical Society in town had of late shot down everything she proposed or opposed. A week in Rome would do her good. I was excited to see her.

"You don't need to come get me," she said, "I can find a cab. They all speak American English, right?"

I had no idea what that meant, but I was more than happy to meet her at the airport.

She spotted me before I saw her, and her squeal brought many a wary traveler to their feet. We hugged and she gave my head a loving rub. "Fuzzy-wuzzy," she said. "I brought you something from home."

"What? What did you bring me?"

But I saw her generous gift even as I asked the question. Brock stood, with his bag in hand, resembling a soldier at attention. Beautiful Brock. A tremor of warmth spread throughout my body.

"I found him outside," said Janey. "Moping around like a lost puppy."

"When she found out she was coming to see you," Brock said, "she insisted on me making the trip as well. I liked that idea."

He was as handsome as ever, though I couldn't say he looked the same. His smile was now a shade darker and more melancholy. Much more authentic than I had ever seen it. As for myself, my heart was about to explode in applause.

"Missed you," he said. He wrapped his arms around me and we held like that for a still, quiet series of moments. I took in his scent and nuzzled into his neck. Perhaps this was too affectionate a show for an airport... but everyone else could go to hell.

We found a taxi to drive us back to my place. The three of us fit cozily in the backseat of the cab, with me in the middle. Just this once I did not mind the lack of personal space. Janey asked questions about my life in Rome—and it did seem a life now, not just a vacation. Any plans for further European travel were forfeit. She listened earnestly to my amateur tour guide schtick as we passed sights I thought would be of interest. From Brock I heard very little. Only an occasional breath of what sounded like satisfied relief. The kind one gets before they burst into happy tears. As I explained to Janey the difference between gelato and ice cream, I felt Brock's fingers cautiously seek companionship from my own. We held hands the rest of the way.

Though Janey thought my new abode was charming, it was perhaps too earthy for her tastes. This was not a surprise. Janey was all about preserving decrepit historical sites; she just didn't want to stay in one. Brock would stay with me, but Janey decided she would get a hotel room. This was the best decision for all of us, for more than one obvious reason. Cassie and Vera got her a place near their own spacious living quarters, and once that was done, Brock, Janey and I set off for some sightseeing.

We wandered in and around the Pantheon. Janey kindly gave Brock and me some alone time as she walked around the architectural marvel, taking pictures on her new camera and scouring the stalls outside for things to take back to Adbury as souvenirs and gifts. Brock stood in the center of the Pantheon, staring up through the great opening in the ceiling. A flawed masterpiece of architectural engineering still standing after centuries; a survivor of wars, gods, and tastes.

He must have felt me studying him as he himself studied the hole in the ceiling. But how could I help myself? My eyes had been introduced once again to the most beautiful man I had ever known. This was a beauty beyond the physical. I knew that now. He was, inside, a wounded thing. That, coupled with whatever chemical reaction makes one person love another with such specificity, made me, at that moment, content to do nothing but look at him and damn the Pantheon.

"Frances is upset with you," he said, still staring up and out, the light from above touching him gently. "She went into quite a fit when she was told you had no plans to finish the book. Her poor secretary locked himself in the bathroom for an hour to get away from her."

"I imagine she'll want the advance back."

"No. I don't think you've heard the last from her about the subject. She wants a book, and she loves your writing."

"She does not. She barely seems to tolerate it."

He gave me a sly look. "She *loves* your writing. Anything she told you otherwise is a big lie."

His face lost its emotion. Or rather, it lost its lines. The skin went as smooth as marble, and it was a heavy look on him.

"Dad died," he said.

"I'm sorry."

"You know…." He fumbled, trying to construct the right words for something he was desperate to say. "I don't want you to think I'm a hypocrite."

"I don't understand what you mean."

"All my talk about you getting out of your box, out of your comfort zone. I don't want you to think I didn't recognize I was in my own. But I was trying to get out of it. That was my whole point when I invited you that weekend to the cabin. I was trying to start something new."

"But?"

"But then... I fell back into my old ways. I saw my dad, how my mom cared for him. I felt the guilt. I never wanted to be responsible for anyone's happiness like that. I just didn't think I had it in me."

"I would never ask you to be responsible for my happiness."

"But you wouldn't need to. I know I hurt you after that weekend. I know that avoiding the topic of what happened—and it was *wonderful*—I know avoiding telling you how wonderful it was hurt you, and I'm so sorry." His eyes were watery and his voice was cracking. "Because I fell in love with you that night. I mean, I was most likely already in love with you, but that night sealed the deal."

We moved along the walls of the Pantheon, seeking a bit more privacy. I wanted to leap and shout and cry "Yee-haw!"

"When I heard that you had left for here," he continued, "I was a zombie, going through my days on autopilot. It wasn't until Dad died that I woke up. The wake was held at the cabin. I tried to grieve with my family, but...." He shrugged and looked at the floor. "I found myself thinking of you, wishing you were there with me again. The next morning when I got up, I decided to go for a swim in the lake. I just decided it. For no reason at all. I went down to the dock, pulled off my boxers, and just dove in." He laughed. "The water was freezing and I nearly drowned again."

"Oh my God!"

"There was no one there to help me this time. And honestly, I had the idea to just... *sink*. But then I thought of you. And I thought of your book. And I thought of when we first met. And everything you had ordered on the table when we first met. And somehow I managed to rise up and get back on the dock. The sun was just up and I lay there on my back, lungs exhausted, and I smiled. I thought of you and I smiled. That was last week. I called Janey and she told me she was coming here. What was I to do but tag along?"

"You followed me around the world?" I was staggered by the idea.

He looked up once more to the hole in the Pantheon. "I think every home needs a big hole in its roof, don't you? What a brilliant idea. One wouldn't feel so… bound."

I leaned over and rested my head on his shoulder, if for a few brief seconds. We were looking up to the light together.

That night, after having seen Janey to her hotel room, Brock and I made love. It was the first time I could honestly say that. Of course, it was love before. Only now it was named as such. It was tender and took its time. As if… as if love was a great blanket we were slowly unfurling through the night, appreciating every stitch and every thread. Every intricate and unique pattern. We kept ourselves warm wrapped up tight in it.

I WAS back at the airport the very next day, waiting on Lucille. How many times had I waited on my mother when I was young: after school, at the store, after a movie. Waiting, irritated and restless, hoping she had not forgotten me or that I would not, again, need to find a pay phone and call home. And there were times I would have to keep calling home every few minutes because she simply wasn't there to answer, having gone to this store or that. I even walked home a few times, finally reaching the front door a couple of hours later. The surprise and guilt on her face made my constructed rant—the curse words and indignation I had built with every stop home—impossible to deliver.

But now, in the airport, I waited on her gladly. And I was certain, for the first time, she would show up. I had paid her way, after all, with my little nest egg, and Lucille was not about to lose her chance to see Italy, to be one of the worldly people she admired. She was so excited that I had called and invited her over that she completely forgot about the ironing she was doing at the time and burned a hole through her favorite blouse.

"Well, shit," she said. "Oh, well. I'll just buy me a new one. *In Italy!*" Then she squealed and squealed. I laughed.

Brock waited with me in the airport. He didn't seem into sightseeing at all—though he had been to Rome before, so that might have accounted for some of his lack of touristic zeal. He was perfectly happy to go where I went, do what I did, even if that meant playing the tour guide to Lucille and Janey. I had never been happier.

We sat across from each other at a table in an airport café. You wait for your loved ones these days. We all wait. Bombs and trust issues. Family and terrorists. Brock grinned and nodded at something over my shoulder. "There's a woman reading your most recent book at a table over there."

"Oh God." I squirmed. I wanted to look, but I couldn't. "Is she enjoying it?"

"Hard to say. Look for yourself."

"I can't." But curiosity poked at my shoulder until I slowly turned around to address it.

A woman in her late thirties, African American, average weight, dressed in sixties chic, was nearing the end of my book,

Trouble Trouble Trouble. She held it by the spine over her crossed legs. She wasn't looking up; she wasn't getting distracted by the business going on around her, which was a good thing. That meant at least my words were holding her interest. But as to whether she was actually enjoying the book, I could not be certain. I was becoming a bit on edge as I watched her. As if I were nominated for an award and she was just about to announce the winner. My stomach began a vacant rumble.

I watched her for a good cluster of minutes, and had yet to see her smile. "I did write a comedy, didn't I?" I said to Brock.

Was this a vicious review in the making? A disappointed stack of sentences I was going to stumble upon one day on Goodreads or Amazon? Would I now have a face to put with every poor review, whether she wrote it or not?

But then, to my great relief, the woman smiled. And it wasn't just any smile. It was glorious, radiant. It was God smiling down from on high. She nodded her head in approval and hesitantly shut the book, breathing a reader's sigh. That wonderful inhale/exhale reaction one does after finishing a book that has somehow touched you. Completion. Inner peace. Separate peace.

I turned back to Brock, feeling quite unexpectedly, once again, like a writer.

"She liked it," he said.

"Seems so," I replied.

And then, as if my inner cheers were vocalized, I heard the high-voiced squeals of my mother, Lucille, as she came from the terminal and caught sight of me at the table. Her arms were stretched high in the sky, jangling with bracelets; her hair (sculpted at the hometown beauty parlor and then maintained every hour on flight, I'm sure to the irritation of many) was as obedient as a small, well-trained dog atop her head; and her outfit was befitting the "event" that a plane trip was for her. Not formal but never casual.

"One should always look one's best on a plane," she had said to me long ago. "You're not getting on some filthy bus to do the shopping. You're *going* somewhere! When I was a young thing growing up in the hills, getting on a plane was as good as a ride at a theme park."

She immersed me in her perfume and kisses, and then did the same to Brock. "I'm so excited! I'm so damn excited!" she said. "Aren't you excited? I kept telling the man next to me on the plane how excited I was. Show me everything!"

"We will," I promised. "But let's get you settled in first, okay? I got you a room—"

"You didn't need to do that!"

"At the Hyatt."

"But I'm so glad you did!" She took hold of our arms and pointed her nose to the sky. "Come on, boys. Get my luggage."

We had a hell of a time keeping up with her strut.

FOR my party, my get-together, my jingling and mingling of past and present and hoped-for future, the weather was perfect. There was, as I had expected, a chill in the air, but everyone dressed accordingly. Good wine and conversation did the rest. The doors to the garden (which by this point I had come to see as but another room of my home) were flung wide open, allowing a free flow of guests and music in and out. White Christmas lights were draped among the trees and the bushes, and music played like a steady undercurrent. Roberto, who had a knack for picking up the hottest new tracks from his nights working at the nightclub, brought over a CD player and a large selection of music. Everyone took their turns as DJ.

The food was served buffet style. There wasn't room enough in the garden for a table to seat all of us—the Odd Assortment and guests. And it was very good food. Much better than anyone expected, though they would never admit to that. Every bit of it was made by Gio's mother, Anna, an Italian who lived and worked in the States but was back in Rome on vacation and to visit with family.

The fire pit just below the steps served as the heart of the party. Laughter sparked from there all evening, as bright and glowing as if logs were being continuously pitched into the blaze. I introduced Janey, Brock, and Lucille to the rest of my merry band of heathens and heretics. My idolators and adulterers. They slid right in. Curtis, who arrived looking for the most part like his old self in khakis (but with a purple sash in place of a belt) pulled me aside after he had met Brock.

"Very nice," he said. Then he nodded toward Marco and Roberto. "And I see you've brought presents for me." His eyes shone even as the sky's light dwindled. We were where we were supposed to be now. We were friends.

Janey approved of this change in our status. "He's not boring anymore," she said, surprised, drinking from a fine piece of crystal Anna had brought. "Look at him. Who knew he just needed to get away from you?"

I called her a bitch, and she agreed.

Curtis had warmed up to Roberto very quickly. Roberto, in his mere straps of leather that were symbolic of a shirt and a tiny pair of shorts, was helming the music as he flirted with Curtis. He played with Curtis's choir-boy haircut like it was the cutest thing he had ever seen. And, luckily, Curtis knew a bit of Italian, so there was at least primitive discourse.

Lucille was a hit with Cassie and Vera. They were apt to show her the ways of whatever eccentricities they could. She was all too eager for the schooling. Soon she was even laughing like them, loud and throaty, her slight country twang as audaciously apparent as her gold hoop earrings. She was having more fun than I can ever remember her having back in Adbury. It was going to be hell trying to get her on a plane back to the States. They'd have to call in the military, I was certain of it.

There were a few others from the Odd Assortment there as well. The deviants and artistic devils I had met in Rome. Veronica showed up, gothic and sarcastic, an emulation of Dorothy Parker by way of Louise Brooks. I could guarantee even then that she was going to inspire a character in some future writing endeavor. Sweet, shy Gio, with his stern mother Anna's watchful blessing, was having quite a go at continuing to woo Marco. And even Bradley Homlick, self-loathing and self-loving at once, accepted the invitation I sent to him and showed up in a red-and-white kimono. He was standoffish at first ("I was just in the area, you see. Just in the area and I thought I'd stop by."), but once surrounded by the fearsome foursome of Vera, Cassie, Lucille, and Veronica, he was soon giggling naughty jokes to any ear that would listen. And he even thanked me for the invitation. That was something I did not expect.

"I'd like to make a toast," I said further on into the evening as the party was in full gallop. Roberto turned the music down and everyone hushed and gathered around the fire pit. "I didn't know what to expect here," I began. "To be honest, when I first arrived in Europe—in Austria—I thought I had made a big mistake. I had run here, you see, to escape… things." I gave Brock a wink. "I know now I shouldn't have run. That wasn't the answer. But at the time it felt right. My writing was going nowhere. Unfortunately, that's exactly where it is right now." Pleasant laughter from the group. "But if I hadn't come here…. In Austria, I met two wonderful ladies."

"That's us," Vera said. She and Cassie stood together, Cassie's arm draped over Vera's magnificently dressed shoulders.

"Yes. That's you. And you introduced me to some others like you. Fabulous artists; filthy, dirty sex fiends; and old friends I had not met yet. I understand now I have not been truly living until recently. I have taken no chances in my life. I have been boxed. I have been controlled."

I saw a tear glisten on Lucille's face, and then realized that I, too, was crying.

I continued. "I was lonely. I was afraid to let go of what had shaped me and my life. But when I finally did, you were all there. Every one of you. So, thank you, and I love you. Cheers!"

"Cheers," they all chimed.

We had barely had time to drink our toast when a voice boomed from the open doors. "Mr. Brandish!"

Standing there in her giant clog shoes and as stern as I had ever seen her was, to my astonishment, Miss Frances Barlow.

"Who invited her?" Brock quipped.

I could not hide my surprise. I made my way to the doors. "Miss Barlow," I said with an undercurrent of shocked laughter. "Won't you join the party?"

"I will *not*. I simply came to collect what's due me. To get your book." Her eyes pinned me to the spot.

"Miss Barlow," I said, trying desperately to sound more soothing than condescending. "I told you: that book is done with. It was going nowhere. You can't deny that. You were right. The zombies were a silly idea. What are you doing in Italy?"

"I just told you. I came to collect your—*my* book."

"How very Reaper-like of you."

"I won't leave without it, Mr. Brandish. I have traveled halfway around the globe for that book, so it better be worth the trip."

By this time a low hum had commenced behind me as my guests gossiped and giggled about what was going on. I tried to keep it a private conversation, but in present company, you'll understand how that was an impossibility.

Brock approached us and put an arm over my shoulder. I breathed in his scent and was at once comforted. "Hello, Frances," he said.

"Hello, Brock," she said, though her eyes never left mine. "So? Where is it? Go get it. I'll wait."

"You came all this way for a book that was only ever half-finished?"

"I take contracts seriously, Mr. Brandish."

"You like me," I teased. "You like my writing, and you like me."

"I don't see how that is relevant, Mr. Brandish. I'm simply—"

"Admit you like me, Miss Barlow. Admit it."

She stood as still as a stone wall, seemingly impenetrable. I was beginning to think she was trying to make my head explode with her stare. Finally, she exhaled and made a great, exhausted clack with her tongue against the roof of her mouth. Her face gave up some of its severity. "Oh, for heaven's sake!" she exclaimed. "*Yes*. I like your writing. It's highly entertaining. Why would I have been hounding you so hard if I didn't like it? And you owe me a book, Mr. Brandish!"

"Well, good then." I straightened my back and puffed out my chest. "I'll write you a book, Miss Barlow. But I do have a condition."

Her stern face returned. "What condition?"

"Call me Logan, and stay for a drink."

"That's two conditions." She looked around, sizing up the goings-on. "But neither of them do I find particularly objectionable."

"Do we need to draw up a contract?"

"No, Logan. Not tonight. And you can call me Frances." She started down toward the party.

"Roberto," I shouted. "Get a drink for my friend Franny."

She turned around with a pointed finger. "I will kick you in the balls if you call me Franny again."

Laughter and open arms from the crowd. A new oddity is inducted into the Assortment.

Brock kissed me hard on the mouth and pressed his chest to mine. "So?" he asked in a manner that queried *what now*.

"So," I replied. "I guess this is Chapter One."

ERIC ARVIN resides in the same sleepy Indiana river town where he grew up. He graduated from Hanover College with a bachelor's degree in history and has lived, for brief periods, in Italy and Australia. He's survived brain surgery and his own loud-mouthed personal demons.

Visit his blog at http://daventryblue.blogspot.com/.

Also from ERIC ARVIN

http://www.dreamspinnerpress.com

www.ingramcontent.com/pod-product-compliance
Lightning Source LLC
Chambersburg PA
CBHW070017260626
47159CB00005B/1845